## Also by Valerie Hobbs

# ANYTHING
## BUT
## ORDINARY

# ANYTHING BUT ORDINARY

VALERIE HOBBS

Frances Foster Books

Farrar Straus Giroux / New York

*A great big thank-you to the talented and gorgeous Divas:*
*Ellen, Lee, Mary, Robin, and Thalia*

Distributed in Canada by Douglas & McIntyre Ltd.
Printed in the United States of America
Designed by Irene Metaxatos
First edition, 2007
1  3  5  7  9  10  8  6  4  2

www.fsgkidsbooks.com

Library of Congress Cataloging-in-Publication Data
Hobbs, Valerie.
Anything but ordinary / Valerie Hobbs.— 1st ed.
    p.  cm.
Summary: Bernie and Winifred have been in love since they were
fourteen, but when Winifred goes away to college in California and
Bernie stays in New Jersey things change for the two of them, and each
must try to forge an identity separate from the other.
ISBN-13: 978-0-374-30374-7
ISBN-10: 0-374-30374-6
[1. Identity—Fiction.  2. College students—Fiction.  3. Universities
and colleges—Fiction.  4. Interpersonal relations—Fiction.
5. California—Fiction.]  I. Title.

PZ7.H65237 An 2007
[Fic]—dc22

2006040851

For Janine

# ANYTHING
# BUT
# ORDINARY

# ONE

When he was fourteen, Bernie Federman fell in love. And he never fell out. Except once, almost. But that was four years and a lifetime later. By that time Winifred (she was calling herself Wini) had become somebody he hardly knew anymore. An ordinary girl.

When he was thirteen, Bernie Federman moved with his parents from Clinton to Pittstown, only half a thumb away according to the map of the great Garden State, but an alien country to Bernie's heart. At Pittstown Middle, two thousand strong, he knew not one person. From the first day, he was a back-row boy, wedged between the makeup girls and the gangsters. Or, in his honors classes, between the brains and the worker bees, when he himself was neither one. Every weekday morning he would have to endure his mother's sad puppy-dog eyes as she handed him his mayonnaise sandwiches—all he could manage to swallow—in a neatly folded paper bag, and watched him trudge out to the bus like he was going to the dentist for a tooth extraction. "It'll get better, hon," she'd say every morning. "Wait and see."

His mother was strong and gentle and funny. She made Bernie laugh, even when he didn't feel like it. Like a best friend, she believed in him. But was she right? If he waited, would things really get better?

* * *

When he was thirteen, Bernie Federman had no idea who he was. Was he the clone of Magnus Morris, his maternal great-great-grandfather, the famous inventor (a brain) who made and lost a million dollars before the age of twenty-three? His mother said he was. Or was he simply the son of a man who worked in a tire shop from six a.m. until six p.m., and was snoring in his La-Z-Boy halfway through *Wheel of Fortune*?

* * *

In the eighth grade other kids seemed to know who they were. They were "into" things. Skateboarding, soccer, Xbox, iPods. Clubs. Eighth grade seemed to be a time for joining clubs. Bernie was a reader and a pretty good chess player, but Pittstown Middle didn't have a Readers' Club or a

Chess Club. Playing chess meant you were a nerd, but there wasn't a Nerds' Club either.

He almost decided to start one. His English teacher, Mrs. Nelson, mentioned one day after announcements that anybody could start a club. All you needed was a constitution and a teacher to agree to be the club's adviser. A rash of clubs popped up—the Harry Club (a sort of readers' club, though the only thing the members read was *Harry Potter*); the (all girl) Fashionistas; Three Sheets to the Wind, a sailing club that had to change its name when the adviser said it had "an unfortunate connotation." Everybody funneled into one club or another, all except for the International Club, which had one lone member: Winifred Owens.

Winifred was a front-row girl, one of those with a pop-up arm. No matter the question, Winifred had the full and complete answer. Bernie could tell that she was about as popular at Pittstown Middle as the cafeteria meat loaf, except of course with teachers like Mrs. Nelson.

"What a fine idea, Winifred!" exclaimed Mrs. Nelson when Winifred proposed the International Club. "Let's see a show of hands. Who would like to join Winifred's club?"

The result was predictable. But Winifred never gave up, not when she suggested the Journaling Club, the Renaissance Comedy Club, or the Live Poets' Society. And nobody, not one kid, signed up.

Then one day Winifred Owens came to school wearing

what looked like an olive on her head, a green knit hat with a bright red pom-pom. That was bad enough. But when she proposed the Green Hat Club, even Mrs. Nelson lost her patience.

"Now, Winifred," Mrs. Nelson said, "of what possible social significance is a Green Hat Club?"

That was when Winifred lost her cool. With a face red as her pom-pom, Winifred stood up and rattled off all the names of the other newly formed clubs—the Jim Carrey Club, Bling Bling on Mondays, the PBJs (members had to have names that began with one of those revered three letters). She saved for last the Fashionistas, all six members of which had worn shocking-pink boas that day and sat in a bunch like a chummy family of flamingos.

"Social significance, Mrs. Nelson? Social significance?" By that time, Winifred was on the verge of tears and her voice shook dangerously. "Popularity, Mrs. Nelson. *That's* what clubs are all about. Don't you know that?"

Then Winifred nodded her head very firmly, just once, and sat down.

She stopped raising her hand in class. And every day, she came to school wearing her green hat with the bright red pom-pom. After a while the kids stopped laughing at her, poking fun, playing catch with her hat, or whinnying like horses (Whhhhinifred! Snort Snort!) whenever she appeared in the cafeteria. After a while it was as if Winifred Owens had become invisible.

Which is exactly how Bernie Federman felt.

It took him a couple of weeks after the Winifred–Mrs. Nelson confrontation to find the right hat, the almost right shade of green, though he couldn't find one with a pom-pom. The hat he finally found, on a 99-cent-sale table at Kmart, could have won, hands down, an ugly-hat contest. It was more puke green than olive green and had a long green tail. The minute he stuck it on his head, Bernie Federman knew something about himself that he hadn't known before. He had a big heart, so big it wasn't afraid to stick up for the most unpopular girl at Pittstown Middle.

* * *

The next day, carrying his bag of mayonnaise sand-wiches, Bernie walked straight to the cafeteria table where Winifred was sitting alone as usual. "Mind if I eat my lunch here?" he said.

Winifred didn't look up from her book. "No," she said. But when he sat down and opened his lunch bag, she stopped reading and glanced at him. "Why are you wearing that stupid hat?"

"Why are you?" he asked.

She shrugged.

"There's nothing on that sandwich," she said. "It's just bread."

He shrugged. He chewed.

She read.

"It's not really a club," she said after a while.

"What?"

"The Green Hat Club. It's not really a club."

"We could write a constitution," Bernie said.

Without comment, Winifred took out her green three-subject spiral notebook and flipped it open. She read aloud the words as she wrote them: "We the members of the infamous Green Hat Club—"

"—in order to form a more perfect union," added Bernie, who had once memorized the entire Bill of Rights for fun—

"—do hereby demand," said Winifred, "freedom from tyranny and bad taste, unlimited library book checkouts, and a special holiday for Green Hat members who are also on the Honor Roll."

"Two holidays for members on the Honor Roll," said Bernie, who knew Winifred would agree.

They met every day at the cafeteria table that now was Bernie's as well as Winifred's. For the first time since his uneventful arrival to the eighth grade, Bernie Federman became visible. Laughable, teasable. Then, finally, gladly, invisible again.

By that time, he and Winifred were trading favorite books, playing chess, doing anagrams, and talking for hours on the phone or online. Bernie had a best friend. He could eat something besides mayonnaise sandwiches and keep it down. His grades went up, way up. Bernie Federman was happy.

# TWO

It wasn't as if they were exactly alike, he and Winifred. She was cultured, he was anything but. Mrs. Owens spoke French and played the bassoon. Professor Owens spoke French, played the viola, and taught dead languages at the university. They weren't snobs—they seemed touchingly grateful that their Winifred had "a little friend to play with"—but they lived a life his mother saw only on TV, on the kind of program that made his father change the channel.

And Bernie and Winifred sure didn't look alike. Winifred was a fireplug, short and square; Bernie was a stork, tall and gawky, his nose like a beak. Winifred's hair was red and frizzy; his hung brown and straight from a middle part and wouldn't stay out of his face. Neither was beauty contest material, which was just fine with them. Beauty contests were "ordinary."

They made a point of being different. It was their bond,

a secret club of two. When all the kids had silver Nikes, they wore Converse sneakers from the thrift store, the more thrashed the better. Instead of listening to the latest pop diva's CDs, they memorized the songs of Broadway musicals. Fads would go through the school like a flu that all the kids were dying to catch: butterfly tattoos, nose rings, Mohawks. For a while it seemed the fad was hooking up, in every kind of way with every body part imaginable. All the time. Between classes, on the way to and from school, sometimes even in class. And so Bernie and Winifred made a vow never to touch each other in public, much less kiss.

Though Bernie wanted to. He wanted to kiss a girl for the experience of the thing; it was a recurring thought that jumped into his head (or his body) and wouldn't go away. Then one day when they were playing Scrabble, Bernie looked up from the seven-letter word he'd almost made and there was Winifred pursing her lips and frowning down at the board. And her lips looked so, well, *kissable*.

Bernie began to plot, inching closer to Winifred at every opportunity, even at the cafeteria table. She didn't seem to notice. Or she noticed and didn't mind. Which made him bolder. The Scrabble words he laid down became clues: if Winifred made a word like "roman," instead of issuing the usual challenge he turned it into "romance." He saved his *l*'s and *o*'s and *e*'s, in case he got a *v*. Once, when he spelled out "caress," a blush appeared on Winifred's neck and turned her cheeks bright pink. But she wouldn't look up from the board, and neither would he.

* * *

It took the predictable to make it all happen: the Freshman Howdy Dance, a walk home under a lopsided moon, the fact that her parents had (probably on purpose) left the porch light off.

Bernie and Winifred weren't going to go to the dance at first. Of course they weren't. Wasn't it about the most ordinary thing a freshman could do? But neither one could stop talking about it, and each secretly wanted to go. Then it hit them both at the same time: what if they could go as *something*, as somebody extraordinary? Bernie rented a tux with tails at the costume shop, complete with a shiny black top hat; Winifred bought a silver gown with sequins (plus a padded bra that Bernie bounced off several times while dancing), and they went to the prom as Fred Astaire and Ginger Rogers. The Owenses splurged on the white stretch limo and the driver, a student in Professor Owens's class, who let them walk the last three blocks home while he followed, keeping a nice distance behind.

The kiss was extraordinary. Not good, because how could it be? Neither of them had any practice. Their braces bumped, their lips touched and then sort of stuck together.

What was extraordinary was that Winifred was willing. If anything, more willing than Bernie. She reached up and put her arms right around him; he wrapped his arms around her, and for five minutes, maybe eight, they stood like statues, kissing. Trading spit, more or less. But extraordinary. He and Winifred kissing. Who would have believed it?

They got better at it, of course. Better at talking about it, too, about what to do next, what they would or should do next. They would absolutely save the Big Moment for their wedding night. Because nobody did, by the sound of it.

It wasn't always easy.

Sophomore year they began riding their bikes out to an abandoned rock quarry where some of the kids went to swim in the hotter weather. They brought along a picnic lunch and Winifred's travel chess set. They ate, they played chess, and they thought about kissing the whole time. Then the kissing wasn't ordinary at all, and Bernie couldn't keep his hands still. They seemed to have an agenda all their own: a voyage to Winifred's breasts.

Winifred borrowed her mother's car and took Bernie to the Backwards Dance. They went as cross-dressers and were immediately told to leave. Instead of going home, they drove out to the rock quarry where they undressed each other in the moonlight. Bernie was awestruck by the beauty that had been hiding under Winifred's thrift-store clothes. That night they touched each other with a sweet tenderness that made them both cry.

* * *

Junior year was the last time Bernie's grade point average was higher than Winifred's. But two great things happened that year that convinced him his mother was right after all: he got voted section leader in band and won second place in the PTA writing contest. He told Winifred that he was going to write a novel someday. He was sure of it.

Bernie called Winifred his girlfriend all the time now. They practically lived at each other's houses, in each other's bedrooms. So that summer when Winifred went off to her family's cabin again, Bernie felt unanchored. Business was better than ever in the dog-walking trade, but all Bernie could think about while the dogs wrapped themselves around his ankles was Winifred. He was sure she'd meet the son of some rich neighbor up there in the Adirondacks and forget all about him.

So when she returned at the end of August and came straight into his arms, he was overjoyed.

In due time, they applied to all the same colleges, starting with the Ivy Leagues. Winifred promised she would turn down any school that didn't offer Bernie a scholarship. With his grades he was certain to get a full ride anywhere he wanted to go, she said. She was as proud of him as she was of herself. They began talking seriously about where they would go, how they would live. In the dorms? Together off campus? Were they ready for that?

For Christmas that year, Bernie gave Winifred half a gold heart with his name engraved on it. Hanging from a gold chain that he now wore was the Winifred half. His father said only sissy men and pimps wore gold chains, but his father worked in a tire shop. What did he know?

What his father knew that Bernie didn't got told to him one night shortly after the New Year. Bernie's mother had cancer, ovarian cancer. Bernie was not to worry, she said. She was going to beat it.

But she didn't, and in two short months she was gone.

\* \* \*

Through it all, Winifred was Bernie's life preserver, his steady beacon off the dark and rocky coast, his faithful guide dog, his homework doer, his hope.

Bernie's father had nobody. From the outside, it seemed to Bernie that nothing much had changed for his father. He went to work at six, he fell asleep in his La-Z-Boy just as before. But there was no one to cook their meals, or wash their clothes, or remind them to take their vitamins. The beds went unmade until the sheets turned gray—had his mother done *everything*?

His father began drinking. First a couple of beers after

dinner, then Jack Daniel's in a juice glass. One morning Bernie found him asleep in his La-Z-Boy at ten past seven in the morning, an empty bottle of Jack Daniel's cradled like a baby in the crook of his arm.

Bernie tried talking to his father about his drinking, but they had never talked much. It wasn't easy to start with such a sensitive subject. So Bernie began cooking dinner—or nuking dinner—so that at least his father would have some food in his stomach. Instead of doing his homework or talking to Winifred, he'd watch his father's stupid television shows. When Bernie was with him, his father switched back to beer. Or he'd sip his Jack Daniel's out of a juice glass instead of the bottle, which was something. They'd sit in the darkened living room, his father in his La-Z-Boy and Bernie on the couch, and miss what used to be—his mother, the background music of their lives that suddenly and forever had stopped playing.

Bernie's grades began to slip. Winifred became alarmed. After all they'd done to separate themselves from the pack, to rise above the ordinary, how awful it would be if Bernie's offers were rescinded. He had to pull himself together, she said. Get a grip.

But he couldn't. He tried, but each time a little voice inside would pop up and ask, "Why bother?" As if it knew what was finally, and irrevocably, true: life was hard and then you died. It didn't matter what you did, who you became, whether you made the very best green bean casserole or not. You might as well buy a La-Z-Boy and work in a tire store as become Donald Trump.

"Wait and see," his mother had said. Well, he did, and look what had happened.

Something about giving in without a fight felt wrong. It didn't even make a lot of sense, but the snickery little voice was more stubborn than Bernie, and it finally won him over. On Tuesday, April 3, his mother's birthday, he stopped going to school. Instead, he hung out in his room reading Jack Kerouac and Zap comics.

Winifred called during second period. "Are you sick? What's wrong?"

She appeared on his doorstep at twenty past three. He wouldn't let her in. The place was a sty. He told her he'd call her. He didn't.

On Wednesday, Winifred showed up with all of their college brochures. They sat on the front steps leafing through the brightly colored pages.

"So what about UC Santa Barbara, Bernie?" she asked. "It's about as far away as we can go."

"I'm not going, Winifred," he said in a voice as deep and grave as Jack Kerouac's.

"Not going where?"

"College," he said. "What good is it?"

Winifred went pale. Her jaw dropped. "What *good* is it? Bernie! What's the matter with you?"

"Isn't college what everybody does?" he said. "Talk about ordinary! We'd get a whole lot more out of hitting the road. Finding out what life is *really* all about."

"Which is what? Starvation? Minimum wage jobs?"

"You are such a snob, Winifred," Bernie said in his world-weary voice. "There are plenty of decent, hard-working people in this world who never went to college. My father, for one."

"You want to work in a tire shop all your life?"

"It's a decent living," he said.

Winifred got up and went home.

Bernie started going to school again, but his heart wasn't really in it.

"What are you going to do, Bernie?" Winifred would ask. "What are you going to do with your life?"

That should have been his first clue: the "you" instead of the "we."

\* \* \*

Bernie began working at his father's tire store every day after school, and sometimes on Saturdays. His father didn't bother him about going to college. Sometimes Bernie thought the snickery little voice in his head was his father's. But his father didn't have a mean bone in his body; really, it seemed he had no bones at all.

As payment for some tires, Bernie's father had taken an

old Ford pickup truck. It was red and covered with splotches of black primer, like an incurable disease. It barely ran, but his father worked on the engine and surprised Bernie by giving it to him for graduation. He put the keys inside a Hallmark card. "For A Dear Son at Graduation," the card said, and had a mushy poem inside. Bernie didn't know whether to laugh or cry.

So the long and short of it was this:

When Bernie Federman was fourteen, he fell in love.

When he was fifteen, he saw his first naked girl.

When he was sixteen, he began to think that someday he might just write a novel.

When he was seventeen, his mother died. Bernie fell from number two in his graduating class to number forty-three, and by graduation had slipped to the muddy bottom. Winifred, of course, was number one.

And now, just one day before Bernie Federman's eighteenth birthday, Winifred Owens, the love of his life, was going to go off to college. Not to Princeton, a mere thirty minutes away, but to the University of California at Santa Barbara, as far as you could go across the country without falling in the water.

And Bernie Federman was drowning.

# THREE

The summer after graduation Winifred's family went abroad. Winifred got to visit all the grand cathedrals, famous museums, cafés, and bookstores of Europe. She flooded Bernie with postcards. "Spent the whole day in the Louvre!" she wrote. Or: "This is where Dylan Thomas fell off a bar stool!" Or: "Shakespeare actually lived here!" Or: "Oxford! Can you believe it?"

She missed him all the time. She called him every week to rave about something that had just changed her life—the rose window at Chartres, *Richard III* at the Globe, Pavarotti singing "Non t'amo piu" in person.

Then came a long pause when she would ask: "What have you been doing, Bernie?"

"Nothing much. Same old, same old."

He was waiting on her porch steps the day she came home, his old red truck parked in front of her house. After greeting Bernie warmly, Winifred's mother and father went inside. Bernie held out his arms and Winifred walked into them. Bernie smelled like home, felt like home, was home. And yet.

And yet . . . what? Well, for one thing, she'd been to Paris and Venice and Barcelona. It changed a person. And now she'd be going off to college where she would change even more.

She sighed and dropped her arms.

"I missed you like crazy," Bernie said, grabbing her hands. "Come on. I've got some Champagne and glasses—real Champagne glasses—in a cooler. Let's go up to the quarry and celebrate being together again."

"The quarry?" Winifred replied, as if she didn't know what he was talking about.

\* \* \*

They began to quarrel. First about little things, like where to go on a Saturday night or what to watch on TV.

"We never used to watch television," Winifred said one night when they were hanging out in her rec room. "Now you know all the shows, all the dumb sitcoms."

"How come you never want to kiss·me anymore?" he asked.

"Do you even read books?" she said.

"Why UC Santa Barbara, Winifred?" he retorted. "I

mean, how far away could you get? Was that the whole point? You can just tell me to get lost, you know. It's not that hard to get rid of me."

"I don't want to get rid of you, Bernie," said Winifred, bursting into tears.

"I know," he said, gathering her into his arms. "I know." But he really didn't. Winifred was changing, right before his eyes, and there wasn't a thing he could do about it.

* * *

For Winifred's last night in town, Bernie made a reservation at Pittstown's fanciest restaurant. They nearly didn't get in. The maître d' looked at them in their thrift-store finery for a full three minutes as if he wasn't sure whether to call the Humane Society or the fashion police. At last he said, "Come this way," and led them to a small table at the very back of the dining room, next to the ladies' restroom.

Bernie wolfed down his seared sea scallops. "Wow!" he managed to say between bites. "This is great!"

Winifred, who had eaten at Le Train Bleu, barely touched her duck à l'orange.

Neither dared to bring up the subject of tomorrow, even though they both thought about nothing else. Until Winifred couldn't stand it anymore.

They had just gotten into the truck when she said

breathlessly, as if she'd been saving it up, "Maybe you shouldn't come to the airport tomorrow, Bernie."

Bernie swallowed hard. "Why not?"

"It will just be too sad, saying goodbye and all."

"Okay," he said at last, over the lump in his throat. "If that's what you want."

"It's not what I *want*," she said. "It's just better for both of us. My whole family will be there. Grandparents, aunts, uncles, the whole scene."

Bernie glanced at Winifred, relieved to see the tears that were streaming down her cheeks.

"Let's go up to the quarry," he said. He heard the pleading note in his voice but could do nothing about it. All summer long, he'd dreamed of being there with Winifred again. It was what kept him going through all the stupid tire changes, all the dreadful TV dinners with his father. He kept seeing in his mind, half crazy with boredom, how beautiful, how spectacularly beautiful she was in the moonlight. He began to believe there was a chance she would change her mind about the Big Moment (he already had). After all, they were just kids when they made up their rule of waiting.

"I don't think so, Bernie," said Winifred. "I'm leaving really early and—"

"Never mind," said Bernie, as quickly as he could get it out. He felt his ribs closing around his poor battered heart. "It's okay. Really."

He walked her to her door as if it were their first date. When he kissed her, he felt her lips shaking. Dying inside, he kissed her forehead and turned away.

\* \* \*

Winifred's eyelids were swollen and red in the morning. Her mother made a cold compress out of a washcloth and told her to lie down on the couch. Was she all packed? Her father would take her suitcases out to the car.

"Suitcase," said Winifred.

"Just one?" said her mother.

Winifred shrugged.

When the extended family arrived, chattering and congratulatory, Winifred did her best to live up to the moment. At the small commuter airport, she hugged each one of them and never shed a tear. It wasn't until she saw them waving from behind the chain-link fence from her seat on the tiny plane that she let herself fall apart.

The plane began to taxi. She blew her nose and smiled back at the flight attendant, a woman not much older than Winifred. Forty minutes and Winifred would be boarding another plane in Newark, and then it was five hours to Los Angeles, where she would catch another plane like this and head to Santa Barbara. She couldn't cry the whole time. She was going to college. At last!

"But why Santa Barbara?" Bernie had kept asking.

"I told you. I want to study nanoscience," she'd said. "It's the hot new field."

Then she'd added that she was tired of cold weather.

After that, she'd just put him off with vague reasons, then silly reasons, and finally he gave up asking.

Why Santa Barbara? For the nanoscience, that was true, and all the Nobel Prize winners. But now Winifred had another reason, an even stronger motive. She needed to grow up. Grow away from Bernie. Bernie with his "new" glass-half-empty philosophy of life. Could it be—dare she even think it?—that she didn't love him anymore?

Winifred looked out the window as the plane began to gain altitude. There in the dry creek bed not far from the runway sat a figure on its haunches, perhaps a homeless man. Beside him, a string of white rocks was arranged to spell in huge crooked letters—I LOVE YOU WINIFRED!!!

"Bernie!" she cried, just as he lifted his arm to wave.

# FOUR

Bernie drove home in a fog, the dawn of an ugly truth just beginning to push its way through. He parked his truck, leaving his backpack on the seat. Inside, the house had the distinct feeling of a place that nobody had ever lived in, cold and still. He went upstairs. He sat on his bed and stared out at the rest of his life, the life that had Winifred right at its center.

Did Winifred even know what she was doing? She'd be lost in college without him. She didn't know how to make friends. Her look was all wrong. She snorted when she laughed. She blushed. Often. Her strong suit had always been her intelligence. But how was that going to help her make it through college?

Was he losing his mind? Intelligence was everything once you got to college. When Winifred shot up her hand in class, nobody was going to scoff behind her back—at least he didn't think they would. You had to be an adult when you went off to college, or at least pretend to be one. Winifred was going to shine.

Still, she *needed* him. He helped guide her through the minefield of their peers the way she'd led him through the quagmire of his grief. She just didn't remember how much she'd always leaned on him. She'd taken him for granted.

But then there was that other thought that had begun to nag at him: he'd let Winifred down. (His mother would have said he'd let himself down, too, but that was something else not to think about.) Winifred had been heading for college since the first grade. Bernie had let his grades tank without a second thought. Traded in his future—their future together—for a La-Z-Boy life.

What a jerk he'd been.

*   *   *

He got up and trudged back down the stairs. He stared for a while at a framed photograph of his parents taken on their wedding day (his mother looked sweet and hopeful, his father looked like he'd been given electroshock therapy). He went back out to his truck and drove to the tire shop.

His father was at the counter doing an invoice when Bernie entered. He looked up, surprised. "I thought you weren't coming in to work today."

"I'm not," said Bernie.

His father went back to the invoice. "What do you need?"

Bernie shrugged. "Can we go get a cup of coffee or something?"

His father looked up again, this time with a frown. "What's wrong?"

"Nothing. Can't we just, you know, *talk?*"

"Uh, sure. Sure. Wait just a minute till I finish this."

Bernie watched his father carefully printing all the required information. He wouldn't get a computer, though Bernie assured him he'd save a lot of time. And time was money, as his father liked to say. A lightbulb hanging from the ceiling illuminated the bald spot in the center of his father's head. It made Bernie feel sorry for him all over again.

They walked silently to the corner with their hands in their pockets, tall Bernie and his average-size father. Inside Starbucks his father frowned up at the board of exotic drink offerings as if trying to solve the riddle of the Sphinx. Then he ordered a "regular-size" cup of coffee, black. Bernie ordered a Caramel Macchiato, Winifred's favorite.

They sat at a small round table, their knees almost touching. His father took a quick sip of his coffee. "Too damned hot," he said, glaring at the black liquid in the decorated paper cup.

"Dad?"

His father looked up.

"Can I ask you something, you know, *personal?*"

His father shrugged. "Sure. You're my son."

"Did you ever love anybody besides Mom? I mean, a woman? Any woman besides Mom?"

His father looked at Bernie through his bloodshot eyes for what seemed like forever. Were there movies running in his head? Was he remembering a special date? Could he see her round face and soft brown curls in his memory as clearly as Bernie could? After a while he said, very quietly, "No. No one but your mother. Sometimes there's just the one, I guess, and she was it."

"I've got to go to California, Dad," Bernie said.

"California? What's in California?"

It struck Bernie how little his father knew about his life, about all the things that mattered to him. What *did* matter to him besides Winifred was a question for another time. He was focused now. He knew what he had to do.

"Winifred's in California," said Bernie. "She's going to school in Santa Barbara." The macchiato was sticky sweet. But he'd known that it would be, and he'd ordered it anyway. Go figure.

"Santa Barbara," mused his father. "You don't say. What made her go all the way out there?"

The question of all questions, not that his father could have known. "Beats me, Dad."

"Tired of the weather maybe," his father said, gazing sorrowfully out the window at a willow tree, dying by the looks of it, and a somber gray sky.

"Do you think the truck will make it?" Bernie asked.

Bernie saw a flicker of fear rise up in his father's eyes, whether for Bernie or for himself, Bernie didn't know. "It's an old truck," his father said. "I didn't pull the heads, you know."

Bernie's mind conjured up an image of his father pulling several decapitated heads out from under the hood of the Ford.

His father began fidgeting with an empty sugar packet, folding it this way and that until he'd made a Star of David. "How long you gonna be there?"

His father's question surprised Bernie. He hadn't thought about that, about coming back. He'd been fantasizing about what would happen only *after* he got to Santa Barbara. He and Winifred under a palm tree, wearing flowered shirts. Not matching, of course. But wasn't that Hawaii, not California?

"I don't know how long, Dad. Not too long." His father looked up; Bernie looked down at his hands, which had already begun to resemble his father's, the nails permanently black. He couldn't deal with the look in his father's eyes, as if his father might be waking up from a coma or emerging like a bear from its cave, tottering toward a world he didn't quite remember.

They walked back to the tire shop. When they got to the door, they shook hands and his father went inside.

Bernie drove the long way home, past all his and Winifred's old haunts: the middle school, the high school, Roma's coffee shop, the Book Den, Goodwill. Then one last place. The zoo, where Winifred had told him she'd be going to UC Santa Barbara.

It wasn't a memorable conversation, if by memorable you meant something you wanted to remember. Particularly his part of it.

"Santa Barbara? I thought you were *joking* about California!" He'd leaped to his feet and begun flinging his arms. "You can't go to California! What are you talking about? What are you thinking? You're not thinking!"

Winifred had let him rant, chewing the inside of her cheek the way she did when she was distressed. Finally, when he began to realize how stupid and desperate he looked, he stopped pacing. "I don't understand"—he was whining now like a three-year-old—"how you could do this to me, to *us*!"

What followed, in Winifred's quiet but firm voice, was a lecture, very little of which Bernie understood. It had to do with nanoscience. Apparently, UCSB was famous for it. Winifred, who he thought all along had been headed for a career in microbiology, was now intent on becoming a nanoscientist. Which meant, as far as Bernie could tell, somebody who studied things so small nobody knew whether or not they were even there. Considering how she'd made him feel, she was going to be very good at it.

Now Bernie gazed out through the pickup's pitted windshield at the litter caught along the fence. The zoo was closed, the iron gates locked tight. Winifred had always loved the zoo and had a family pass. It was just the kind of place no other couple would think of going just to be alone, especially to talk about the future. Now the place looked bleak and empty.

Back at the house, Bernie called the Owenses', got their voice mail, and hung up. He was pretty sure they'd give him the number of Winifred's new dorm, though they were bound to wonder why she hadn't given it to him herself.

He punched 411 and asked a machine for the university in Santa Barbara. After a series of switches, he landed in the lap of somebody from Student Services who said in a take-no-prisoners voice that they were not, under any circumstances, allowed to give out the addresses or telephone numbers of incoming students, or any students for that matter. It was a safety issue, she said.

Safety. That was a whole other thing. He hadn't thought about Winifred's safety until just that minute. How she walked through the world as if she were encased in a bullet-proof bubble. He'd had to grab her arm more than once to pull her back from a city bus hurtling by or a dog foaming at the mouth. (Well, it *looked* like foam.) She had no concept of how dangerous the world was, how it was filled with rapists and terrorists.

She needed him. She *did*.

# FIVE

"Here you go, young lady." Winifred stared from the window of the taxi at the line of cars piled with luggage, all inching toward the six stories of dull brown brick. "San Marcos Hall."

Winifred broke out in a sweat. Her hand was stuck to the door handle. She heard the driver get out and open the trunk. Okay, so she had to open the door and get out, too. This was it, her new home for at least the next nine months. She climbed out of the taxi on shaky legs.

Nine months. Like she was going back into the womb. Wasn't that funny? Hysterical! Well, Bernie would have thought so. But (Winifred reminded herself for the umpteenth time) she had to stop thinking about Bernie. What Bernie would think or say. She was on her own now. No more dark clouds. A Whole New Start. Winifred squared her shoulders. She paid and tipped the driver, picked up her suitcase, slung her backpack over her shoulder, and waded, chin up, into the crowd.

San Marcos Hall looked like a prison compound, but the kids swarming around her seemed thrilled with it. Screaming and laughing like twelve-year-olds at camp, they hauled TVs and computers, suitcases and shiny metallic steamer trunks into elevators and up the concrete stairs. Winifred was shocked. Everybody had come with parents, at least one, plus a pack of wild siblings. Why hadn't she let her mom come with her? What was that whole going-away speech about independence and self-reliance anyway? Too much Emerson and Thoreau, and now she had nobody to help feather her new nest or say goodbye to.

Winifred gave herself a mental kick in the head. Her Whole New Start was going to begin right this minute. She was going to stop being so all-fired stubborn. It was time to open her eyes to new ways of seeing things, new vistas of possibility. She wasn't always right. Even if she was absolutely certain she was right, she was going to keep an open mind. ("Like Swiss cheese?" said the voice of Bernie in her mind.)

A boy wearing a football jersey pushed past Winifred into the already overstuffed elevator, knocking her sideways. The door slid closed. Winifred felt like kicking it. She picked up her suitcase and headed for the stairs.

On the fourth-floor landing, she stopped to catch her breath. She was *so* out of shape. Well, she'd never really been *in* shape. She put "get in shape" on her mental Whole New Start list. The stairwell echoed with hyperexcited chatter. The parents coming down looked like they'd attended a funeral. One father was literally holding his wife up as they made their way down the stairs.

"Honey, stop now. Caitlin's a big girl."

"But she's my *ba*by!" cried the mother, sobbing into a soggy-looking tissue.

By the time she reached the sixth floor, her floor, Winifred was dripping sweat. She wound her way around boxes and trunks, past frantic parents, crying girls, screaming girls, hugging girls. Every room was a hive of activity. Thankfully (and strangely) Winifred's was not—6C was open and nobody was home. Winifred checked for her name on the door, which she found along with three others: Calista Bearden, Victoria Castagnola, and Samantha Gray.

The room was the size of her bedroom at home. Two bunkbeds and four tiny dressers and desks took up nearly every square inch of space. Three of the beds were already claimed and made up. Winifred looked at the remaining bed, an upper bunk, with its striped lumpy-looking mattress and thought about her princess four-poster with its plush pink down comforter. She heard herself sigh. She sounded just like her mother.

*Enough!* Winifred unpacked her plain white sheets, her travel pillow, and a tan fleece blanket. In no time she had made up her bed and filled two drawers of her dresser with her recycled clothes. And that was it. Winifred, student ID number 457865738, was all moved in.

She sat in a patch of sunlight on her newly made-up bed. Through an open window came the tangy, exciting smell of the ocean. And Winifred noticed something less appealing, her armpits. She grabbed a towel, soap, and shampoo and headed for the shower.

As the water pelted her head, Winifred relaxed, and when she relaxed it was impossible not to think about Bernie. Winifred felt the tears rising (she'd already wept in several restrooms, including the closet-sized one on the plane). None of this was right. Bernie was supposed to be here. Or she there.

*Enough!* Winifred cranked off the left faucet. Cold water hit her body like a wake-up call. She'd had it with Bernie. The boy she'd practically grown up with, the kid with all the crazy, funny ideas, the guy who'd stretched her brain, challenged her all those years to be her best and brightest self, had turned into an ordinary person with a dumbed-down mind. Bernie was *supposed* to graduate, like she did, at the top of their class. Bernie was *supposed* to pull himself together. Bernie was *supposed* to be a college freshman.

Bang! Bang! Bang! "Hey! Open the door! Yoo-hoo!" Winifred snatched up her towel and clutched it to her chest. A pack of laughing hyenas was on the other side of the bathroom door. "Come out, come out, whoever you are!" That line pitched them into hysterics. Winifred cringed behind the door, listening to the yips and shrieks and helpless howling of the girls with whom she was destined to share a life.

She couldn't very well camp out in the bathroom all night. Ready or not, it was time to meet them. She wrapped the towel around her, tucking it tightly, and opened the door.

Three faces fell.

"Winnie?" asked the tallest girl, a beyond-gorgeous blonde with a late-season tan, wearing a pair of mini-cutoffs and a black bikini top. Two similarly clad striking brunettes to the blonde's left and right peered at Winifred as if examining a tree shrew.

"Winifred," said Winifred, brushing past. "Now, if you'll excuse me, I'm going to get dressed." Hands shaking, Winifred opened her dresser drawer, grabbed some clothes, and fled back to the bathroom.

"Well, excuuuuuse us!" said the blonde, and they all cracked up again.

Winifred cleared a circle on the steamy bathroom mirror. Her round red face, hair dripping, looked defiantly, then unhappily, back at her. She towel-dried her hair and pulled on a pair of baggy gray sweatpants and a white T-shirt. Then she closed her eyes and, biting her thumbnail, silently practiced a couple of different openers: "Hey, girls! How's it going?" "Hi! Sorry I hogged the bathroom. I'm Winifred." "Hi! I'm the new and improved dry Winifred. Glad to meet you!"

Winifred took a deep breath and opened the bathroom door. "Hey!" she said.

Her roommates were piled onto one bed, curled around and over one another, all talking at once. Nobody turned to look at her. Winifred stood in the middle of the scuffed linoleum floor of 6C, as invisible as she'd ever been in middle school. She felt like an idiot. She dropped her wet towel and dirty clothes on her dresser.

"See ya!" she cried cheerily, and stumbled out the door.

Where was she going? And did it matter? Tears streamed down Winifred's face. This was not a good start. Definitely not a Whole New Start. What was with her anyway? What did it matter if she was called Winnie or Whinny or Mini Winnie (her particular favorite!)? Despite the adolescent behavior of her roommates, this was not middle school. Winifred punched the down button on the elevator. She would go exploring. Walk on the beach. Find the cafeteria. She would not call her parents. She would not even think about Bernie. "Welcome to the University of California, Winifred Owens," Winifred said aloud as the elevator doors opened and out stepped Orlando Bloom.

She stepped into the elevator and, with her finger on the button to keep the door open, Winifred stuck her head back out. She still wasn't sure it wasn't him, the famous movie star. But that was his tousled hair, all right. He'd looked straight at her (and through her) with those same soulful eyes. But he wouldn't be here at a college, would he? He was at least twenty-five, *at least.*

Winifred watched until the Orlando Bloom look-alike took a right turn, straight into 6C. Did *all* the kids at UC Santa Barbara look like movie stars?

The sun was just beginning to set. Instead of heading for the beach, entirely too romantic, Winifred wandered around the campus until she smelled food.

In the cafeteria, Winifred was relieved to find that normal people, kids in all sizes and shades and shapes, had found their way to UCSB after all. She packed her tray with food: macaroni and cheese, ambrosia salad, cheese toast, a taco, apple pie, and a coke. Never a fan of cafeterias, Winifred was delighted at all the choices she could pay for with a simple access card. Food was so . . . so comforting. What were a few more pounds? Skinny girls had skinny minds, Bernie always said.

Bernie again.

What was there to do at night around here? Well, study, of course. But she didn't have any homework yet. She'd have to find something to pass the time. No way would she go back to her room until the hyenas were dead asleep. She'd face them again in the morning, after a good night's rest. Everybody would be in a more charitable mood then, she was sure of it.

As the sky darkened and a few stars popped out, Winifred hiked from one side of campus to the other. What a huge, strange place this was. Nothing matched. One building was Greek Revival, another looked like a shriveled mushroom. She felt like Alice in Wonderland in search of the Red Queen. As a full moon rose into an indigo sky, she sat on the edge of a pool with no water in it. GIFT OF THE CLASS OF 1968 said a plaque affixed to the side. She'd like to have been a student then, when being an individual mattered. Nobody was beautiful then, at least according to the ancient *LIFE* magazines her father had. They had stringy long hair, wore headbands and love beads. Their sandaled feet looked dirty. She and Bernie had done the hippie thing for a while. That was in eighth grade, when *Grease* was the school play and all the girls wore poodle skirts and bobby socks for a month.

Was it all Bernie's fault that she was so different from other girls her age? Now *that* was something to think about. What if he hadn't shown up that day in eighth grade wearing that silly green hat? What if he hadn't constantly encouraged her to be what he said was "herself"? What if her "self" was really just someone else's creation?

Winifred hopped to her feet, inflated with a whole new sense of self, a whole other person to blame for how she had turned out. Bernie Federman. This new sense of self might not know exactly who she was yet, but that wasn't going to stop her. She was smart, she was brave, and she was going to take UC Santa Barbara by storm. In four years when she graduated summa cum laude, she would send a graduation invitation to Bernie, who by then, she supposed, would be a master tire putter-onner. She would have so many friends he'd get lost trying to find her in the crowd. Three baby hyenas were no match for Winifred Owens, no sirree. And Bernie Federman wasn't going to tell her what to do. Not anymore.

But where to go now? The library! A port in any storm. She might as well get to know the place before it was packed with kids. Or maybe it was already packed. Nobody seemed to be anywhere else.

\* \* \*

Winifred awoke with drool running down her chin. The chair was big and comfy. It smelled a little like hippie feet, but that hadn't stopped her from falling asleep over a sociology book picked at random from the shelf. She yawned and got up. The clock over the circulation desk said twenty past eleven. The hyenas had to be drifting in dreamland by now, plotting their next kill.

\* \* \*

Winifred looked up at the sixth floor and, remembering there were two windows to a room, counted over. Just her luck, 6C was one of the dozen dorm windows with the lights on. From the open windows came the thumping beat of rap music.

She turned and began walking again, wishing she'd grabbed a sweatshirt before her grand exit. The air was chilly, much too cold for a place sprouting palm trees. She came at last to the edge of a cliff along which was strung a flimsy wire fence. A bench waiting for lovers looked out at the sea. From below came a gentle shushing of waves. Hugging her goose-bumpy arms, Winifred gazed into space. The moon had laid a rippling yellow scarf across the dark water. It was so beautiful it made you weep.

# SIX

As classes got into full swing, despite Winifred's valiant attempts to interest her roommates in her new and improved self, nothing changed. They didn't ignore her exactly. They were sometimes even polite, but they all looked at her in the same strange way—as if they were constantly surprised she was still there. Calista (the blonde) stared openly at Winifred's ragged cuticles and suggested a certain papaya-based cream; Tory (the booby brunette) actually bounced on Winifred's bed once to see if she "got the good mattress"; but Sam (the too-thin brunette) would smile almost shyly at Winifred now and then if she thought the others weren't looking.

Winifred liked all her classes, especially English 2. Diedre ("I'm just a TA, so don't call me professor, you guys, okay?") looked so young that, at first, Winifred wasn't prepared to take her seriously. That ended the day Diedre led them through a Wallace Stevens poem about blackbirds.

Winifred left the classroom, her mind reeling with ideas about the "absolute intransigence of things" (which, she had to admit, she really didn't understand). Still, she'd been engaged in high-level intellectual combat. She'd even landed a punch. How puny her concerns about acceptance by three very ordinary girls.

Sociology 1 was a whole different trip, held off campus in a defunct movie theater that still bore its original Magic Lantern sign. The professor ("call me Andy, call me anything you want, just don't call me after ten at night") played rock music as the class found seats. "Settle down, brothers and sisters! Let's get this show on the road. Welcome to sOHsh 1—spelled s-o-c."

Andy wore black and strolled the stage with a hand-held mike like a revivalist preacher. But, wow, did he know his stuff! Once again, Winifred was caught up like a simple snowflake in a hailstorm of theories about the actual way that society worked, the deep meaning of things. Bernie would just—

But Bernie wasn't here.

She sent Bernie a postcard, spending hours searching for just the right one. Generic. Upbeat. Impersonal, but warm. Totally non-encouraging, but philosophically generous. She settled for an aerial photo of the campus taken at sunset. Then she slaved over what to say, rehearsing several possible messages on scratch paper. Finally, she decided in favor of what was most true.

*Dear Bernie,*
*I'm sorry.*
*Love, Winifred*

What else was there to say? If she admitted all the rest of it—that she missed him like crazy, that everything reminded her of something they'd done or said or thought or laughed over—well, he'd be here in a heartbeat, dragging his heavy dark clouds behind him, along with all the morbid ideas he thought were so original. Instead of swimming in a bracing sea of actually totally original ideas and theories, she'd be drowning in Bernie's depression.

She scribbled Bernie's address on the card, stamped it, and dropped it in the mail. No way could he see a card like that as anything but what it was, a sad and final goodbye.

Calculus 1, a "filter" class for the premed program, was a little tough, even for Winifred. So most of her study time got spent working formulas over and over in the library's reading room. The dorms, as it turned out, were seldom used for studying, or even for sleeping much of the time. Roving bands of kids would swarm in and out of rooms like carolers at Christmas, bringing cheer, beer (smuggled under baggy sweatshirts), and munchies. She found herself being squeezed out into the hall like a pimple. Out of her own room!

Then, unaccountably, something changed. Winifred had given up trying to have any private time in the bathroom. It was a challenge to undress, and especially dress, under a towel in their crowded room, but all the girls had the same eight o'clock soc class. Calista, Tory, and Sam would sleep until the very last minute, then pile into the bathroom, showering, brushing teeth, putting on as little makeup as they could get away with. Really, it was an impersonal thing, like the locker room at Pittstown High. Even if Winifred happened to drop her towel, she doubted any of the girls would notice the extra pounds that had so quickly stuck themselves to her tummy.

But she was wrong. One morning, two weeks into the quarter, having grunted her way into her Levi's, Winifred turned and there stood Calista, hands on her no-hips, a tiny frown between her amber eyes. The eyes were fixed we all know where. "You're not eating in the cafeteria, are you?"

"Well, sure," said Winifred, shocked that Calista was speaking so directly to her. "Why not?"

"Winnie! You're not serious. The freshman fifteen, girl!"

"The *what*?"

"It happens to everybody who eats the cafeteria food. Mostly girls. They pack on fifteen, twenty pounds their first year. You can't do that to yourself. You've got a round face! A pretty face, I might add."

Calista turned to Tory and Sam, who hung on her every word as if she were delivering the gospel. They nodded solemnly.

Winifred was genuinely puzzled. "But where do you eat? I mean, where else is there?"

Calista shrugged. "Oh, I grab a cup of yogurt at the student store. If I'm being *really* reckless I pick up a nonfat protein shake and sip on it until dinner. Tory, now, she can eat anything she wants, as much as she wants, and not gain a pound."

"It's because I'm Italian," Tory said. "It all goes to my boobs!"

Laughter.

"And Sam, well—" Calista lifted a perfectly plucked eyebrow.

They all turned to Sam, who grabbed up toiletries. "I'm gonna be late," she said. "See ya!" And she was out the bathroom door.

"Don't tell her I told you," Calista said, laying a hand confidentially on Winifred's shoulder, "but Sam's diet is, you know . . ." She stuck her finger in her mouth and pretended to gag. "The old in and out."

Horrified, all Winifred could do was smile weakly. Later she thought she'd been a coward. Surely they all knew how dangerous purging was. Like Winifred and Bernie, Calista and Sam had been friends since middle school (how they'd managed to get a room together was something Winifred hadn't yet figured out). *Best* friends. Didn't Calista care about her best friend's health? If anything, Sam's legs were skinnier than they'd been two weeks earlier, when Winifred first saw them.

Calista's revelation led to several more that Winifred

could happily have done without. As virgins, Calista and Sam had decided to "do" the same boy in ninth grade "as a science experiment," comparing notes afterward. They'd done it with several boys over the years "just for fun." Tory was "technically a virgin," saving herself for the "right guy," some prelaw jock from a wealthy family, preferably from the Northeast. Her boobs, it turned out, weren't food-fed after all; they were a sixteenth-birthday present from her parents.

Mornings, in the bathroom, somebody would pass Winifred a lipstick for her to try. "You've got great hair, Winnie," Calista said once over Winifred's shoulder into the mirror. "All you need is a good cut. I know! I'll treat you to my guy for your birthday!"

*Her guy?* Winifred nearly yelped in mortification.

"He's at Nona's in Montecito. When's your birthday anyway?"

"Not until December," said Winifred, relieved that Calista's guy was only her hairdresser.

"Well, then, an early birthday present. I know! Hey Sam, Tor, how does this sound? A spa day! I'll make the appointments."

Tory and Sam screamed their approval from the bedroom.

"Winnie, my love," said Calista, laying a single finger fairy godmother–like on the top of Winifred's head, "you just leave everything to me."

# SEVEN

Winifred was wallowing like a pink piglet in a deep tub of mud. Her towel-wrapped head had been placed on a lavender-scented pillow, and over her eyes lay some kind of mask-thing that reminded her of Provence. Spa Day, girls' day out, and she was one of the girls.

Her massage had been with a masseur named Patrice. He was French and so charming that Winifred wanted to bolt. Fast. But once the massage began, Patrice was so totally professional that Winifred dropped into the best sleep she'd had since leaving home.

The spa was in a hotel she'd already forgotten the name of, she was so blown away by it all. Especially by the ride over in Calista's silver BMW. With the top down, the girls all sailed down 101, belting out eighties songs at the top of their lungs. Winifred was shocked by how much fun she was having.

After their treatments, the girls regrouped for lunch on

the bistro patio overlooking the ocean. It was a fabulous day, the sky a perfect baby blue. Calista insisted Winifred take the best seat, the one facing the sun-kissed ocean, since she wasn't used to California as they all were.

"To Winnie!" cried Calista, raising her glass of iced tea. "To our new best friend!"

Winifred blushed. "I'd rather be called Winifred," she said meekly.

"But why?" asked Tory. "Spell it W-I-N-I. It's so cute!"

"Well," she said. "I suppose . . ." She whipped her head around. What was *that*? Bernie in the bushes snickering?

After vegetable salads ("no dressing on any of them," Calista ordered imperiously, "and no bread"), they got back into the Beemer and drove downtown. "I hope you brought your charge cards, girls," Calista warned, pulling into a parking space at a small but elegant strip mall. "This place is hot!"

Calista tried on a pair of jeans, Tory a bright-red stretch top. Sam said she felt "too fat to try on clothes today." Mostly the girls ran back and forth finding things for Wini to model—low-cut jeans with embroidered flowers running down each leg, a chartreuse rabbit-fur boa, black boots with witchy toes and heels so high Winifred couldn't walk three steps in them. ("But they're gorgeous!" argued Tory. "Just think how you'll look sitting down! Unreal!")

Winifred left with a whole new wardrobe, her head spinning with unrecognizable pictures of herself wrapped waist to neck in gold angora, her chubby white legs on display beneath a suede miniskirt ("you'll want tights for that," mused Tory).

"Next stop, Nona's," said Calista, backing out of the parking space. "Then it's a double capp for me. I'm shot."

* * *

At Nona's, Winifred went like a car on an assembly line from colorist to washer to hairdresser to the assistant who did the blow-dry. Then it was the manicurist (who also did the pedicure), then the depilator, the exfoliator, and finally the makeup coordinator. It was all a dazzling blur of lights and color, faces popping in and out, consultations in which she had no say.

At last Winifred got to appraise Wini in the mirror framed by Hollywood lights. Her eyebrows had been plucked and dyed black, her lips outlined and filled in with a gloss guaranteed to keep a pout for three hours (unless you were actually to eat). There was blusher and bronzer, three shades of eye shadow and three coats of mascara. Her hair, no longer red, was sleek and black as a seal's coat.

By the end of the afternoon, Winifred was a whole new person. Not exactly the person she had in mind that first night on campus when she'd pledged under a full moon to change her life forever. This was more, she had to admit, an *appearance* thing. Which, when she thought about it, wasn't a *bad* thing. She'd been so behind the times (well, there again, Bernie's influence). She'd just caught up with the other girls her age. Right?

"You are going to kill them at the party!" said Calista when they were back in 6C. Winifred's embroidered jeans and tight-fitting top were laid out on her bed in the shape of her new self. All she would need was a Wonderbra to make actual boobs, Sam promised. Actual boobs!

"Party?" said Winifred.

"It's a frat thing. The usual," said Tory with a bored shrug.

"I'm sorry we didn't invite you before," said Sam in a sugary whisper.

"We didn't think you'd *want* to go," said Tory. "I mean, are you religious or something?"

"Me?" said Winifred.

"Well, the way you study and all!"

"Oh, *that*," said Winifred. And there, with a very Calista-like wave of her hand, went Winifred's study time.

"Girls! Pul-eeze!" cried Calista. "Wini's the only one with soc notes for the midterm. Whoops!" She clasped a hand over her mouth and fluttered her eyelashes.

"Hey, Wini," said Tory, "I hope you don't think today was, like, you know, about getting your notes or something."

"Oh! No!" cried Winifred. "Today was so . . . so fun!"

Calista looked at Winifred blankly, and said, "Today was *work*, girl. I am plumb wiped out!"

Then she cracked up. So did Tory and Sam. And Wini. Wini laughed so hard she nearly peed her baggy pink cotton underpants, which after today she would forswear in favor of her brand-new leopard-print thongs. They'd take some getting used to, but so did this astonishing royal treatment from her roommates. Whatever she'd done or would have to do to deserve it, Winifred didn't know and didn't care. For the first time in her life, her entire life as a girl, she detected in the air the distant but distinct whiff of popularity. It was as heady and irresistible as a drug.

# EIGHT

The picture on the glossy postcard had been taken from an airplane. Sprawled at the ragged edge of a continent was a small city of buildings. UNIVERSITY OF CALIFORNIA, SANTA BARBARA said the bold black script. Bernie's hopes soared as he turned the card over:

> *Dear Bernie,*
> *I'm sorry.*
> *Love, Winifred*

What was that supposed to mean? A measly six words! What was he to make of this?

He flipped the card over again, searching for clues—like if she'd sent a card with a sunset on it, well, then he'd know it was over. But with the sun glittering off that blue, blue ocean, it had to be sunrise.

And love. She had written "Love" when she could just

as easily have signed her name or said "Sincerely" or "Your friend." How could Bernie read Winifred's words as anything but encouraging? She was sorry she'd left him behind. Obviously she missed him.

The fact that there wasn't a return address or a phone number didn't really mean much. Winifred could be absent-minded. So was Albert Einstein!

Nevertheless, it was hard to keep faith on the basis of one flimsy little card, so Bernie threw himself into his work. Seven to five at the tire shop, six to midnight flipping burgers at Fat Boys. Bernie imagined that Winifred was totally overwhelmed. Adjusting to college life, studying nonstop. And it was just possible (wasn't it?) that she'd stumbled into a deep depression, so deep she could only write six words. Clearly the postcard was a call for help.

Bernie started saving money with a vengeance. At the end of his Fat Boys shift, too wired to sleep, he'd e-mail Winifred and tell her all the funny or strange little things that happened in his day. He kept his tone upbeat, didn't whine, didn't beg. He didn't even ask her to answer. His mail never bounced back, which, he told himself, was better than nothing. Three weeks went by. Three long weeks without Winifred. He set a date and marked it on his calendar: October 15. That was the day he would leave for Santa Barbara.

In his free time, what little he had, he read *War and Peace*. The great Russian novel that was meant to keep his mind sharp only knocked him out. What if he wasn't a brain after all? What if he was just an ordinary slob?

On October 15, Bernie carried his duffel and the camouflage sleeping bag he'd had since Cub Scouts downstairs.

He sat down at the kitchen table and tried to write his father a note, a sort of formal goodbye letter. But he couldn't do it. Every attempt sounded like a father giving a son advice, instead of the other way around: don't forget to take your meds, cut back on the drinking. So he called his father at the shop instead.

"Well, be careful," his father said when they'd run out of the few things they had to say. It was what his father always said.

"You, too, Dad."

Behind the wheel of his pickup, Bernie took a long look at the house. It wasn't like leaving the home he grew up in. He'd never set his heart down here, not really. At thirteen your heart was already looking somewhere else, at least his was.

"Goodbye, Mom," he said. Not in his mind but aloud, into the air where her spirit maybe still was.

Cruising along with the big rigs on the highway, Bernie was euphoric. He began to feel grateful to Winifred for shaking up their boring lives. She'd been right, he wasn't going anywhere. Now he was crossing the entire country! Through his stuck-open window, the wind blew his long hair every which way, giving him a feeling of freedom he'd never had before.

Just over the Pennsylvania state line at a gas station, a trucker called him "girlie." "Hey, girlie," he said, coming out of the mini-mart with a steaming cup of coffee. "What year's that little pickup of yours?" Bernie's scalp prickled. He climbed into his truck without answering. But once he was behind the wheel again, he decided it was all in fun. The kind of thing you'd say to a buddy on the road. He felt like a jerk for not answering a simple question.

The pickup was running like a champ. As the sun began to set, Bernie crossed out of Pennsylvania into Ohio. He parked at the edge of a cornfield for the night and, staring up at a single star in a licorice sky, thought: I'm coming, Winifred. Hang on.

He rolled uneventfully through Indiana and Illinois, stopping only for gas and food. It began to worry Bernie how fast his money could dribble away.

Outside Kansas City, Missouri, he bought a crate of apples and for three days he ate nothing else.

When his stomach revolted in Wichita, he bought a loaf of white bread and a jar of peanut butter, which lasted him until Colorado.

Colorado got more exciting. The wind picked up. The sky looked wider and bluer. He and the truck (he'd begun calling her Girlie) began to tackle mountains. At first, Girlie was okay with this. Then she began running a temp. The little red needle on her heat gauge started to climb. His father had told Bernie to watch out for this. Bernie stopped at a scenic overlook to let Girlie cool down. He made a last peanut-butter sandwich, while just outside his windshield a pair of hawks performed aerobatics just for him.

He was gentler with Girlie after that, fed her premium-grade gas though he really couldn't afford to. She was all he had. Until he got to Winifred anyway.

In the middle of Utah, Bernie realized he was talking to himself. Or to Girlie. And that he'd been doing that for some time. He thought about the pioneers who'd lost their minds crossing the desert or, starving, had eaten one another. He couldn't seem to think of good things. He wished Girlie had a radio. What kind of idiot would drive three thousand miles without music?

Well, he hadn't really planned it all out. Like the window that wouldn't roll up, for one thing. He'd told his father he'd get it fixed, but he never did.

Somewhere between St. George, in Utah, and Las Vegas, black clouds boiled up from the flat earth and the wind began blowing the truck sideways. Bernie hung on to the wheel, his heart pounding like a bass drum. Then the sky cracked open and the rain came down. He was soaked straight through his underwear before he knew it, water dripping steadily off his nose.

Near Las Vegas, wet and miserable, Bernie pulled into the Bucking Bronco Motel, and for $34.95 plus tax got a bed, a shower, and a TV. The mattress sagged, the shower turned cold after two minutes, and the TV carried one local channel that ran only highlights of a recent school-board meeting. But for Bernie, it was pure luxury.

That night he dreamed he and Winifred were at the zoo, but it wasn't a good dream. She had somehow gotten locked into a cage with a bunch of monkeys. One was sitting on her shoulder grooming her red hair. "Get me out of here, Bernie," she'd said, seriously and very quietly—he guessed so that she wouldn't hurt the monkey's feelings. Winifred could be like that.

He awoke with a fevered commitment to get to her. Only one more long day on the road and he would be in Santa Barbara. In his mind Bernie saw Winifred dancing toward him through a field of wildflowers, like in that shampoo commercial he used to think was dumb.

At the edge of Las Vegas in a diner, Bernie wasted three dollars playing a nickel slot machine, but the cooked-to-death jumbo hotdog was only two bucks and change. He burped all the way, bumper to bumper, down the Strip. Las Vegas was amazing. New York here, Paris there. He could hardly keep his eyes on the car ahead of him.

Past Vegas, when the desert became endless and boring, Bernie started singing show tunes. He remembered the talent contest he and Winifred hadn't won, though they were clearly the best. Well, at least they knew all the words. He sang "Anything Goes" at the top of his lungs as the tumbleweed tumbled past bits of road trash.

He was five hours, tops, away from a reunion with his love when Girlie began singing, too. First something that sounded like a wheeze, then a high-pitched whistle. Bernie took his foot off the accelerator and coasted to a stop as the traffic whizzed by going eighty, ninety miles an hour, blowing dust.

He got out and lifted Girlie's hood, mostly for something to do. It occurred to Bernie for the first time that nobody in his right mind would cross the desert in a forty-year-old truck unless they knew something about engines. He poked at a couple of hoses and burned his fingers on the radiator cap, which good sense told him to leave right where it was.

He climbed back into his truck to think.

Yeah, so he should have a cell phone. But that seemed like a thing he needed to okay with Winifred first. Cell phones had always been on their list of Life's Most Ubiquitous and Useless Things.

A shiny black pickup the size of a house trailer slid to a halt behind him. As the dust rose, two men in cowboy hats stepped out. The taller of the two walked over with his thumbs stuck in his front pockets. "She aleakin' fer ye, boy?"

"Pardon?" said Bernie.

"Well, come on then. Let's have a look-see."

Bernie scrambled out and lifted Girlie's hood.

The cowboy twisted off her radiator cap. "She's one old gal, ain't she?" he said. Bernie watched the cowboy walk back to his pickup and return carrying a watering can. It was green plastic, exactly like the one his mother had used to water her tomato plants. It looked strange dangling from the cowboy's hand. "That'll hold 'er till the next station, just over the rise," he said as he tilted in the last of the water.

Bernie thanked the cowboy profusely, and offered him a five-dollar bill. The cowboy waved him off. "Save it for a haircut," he said.

Girlie started right up, but after a while she began to wheeze again. Bernie slowed down. Cars began passing him, some of the drivers honking or flipping him the bird. One thing he'd learned: there were all kinds of people in the world, some who helped out, some who wanted to wipe the road with you. Bernie's romantic adventure began to feel like a joyless journey. He was tired of driving. He doubted he'd make it to Santa Barbara before nightfall. He really had no idea how to locate Winifred, but he wasn't going to spot that red hair in the dark. He was going to have to spend another night on the road.

On the outskirts of Barstow—could this depressing burg really be California?—Bernie parked behind a boarded-up gun shop. He slept all night with one ear cocked. Near dawn he awoke to the sound of coyotes—and they *were* coyotes, not just dogs—yipping in the distance. In the not-too-distant distance. He jumped out of the pickup bed into the cab, and drove off.

With a six-pack of Krispy Kreme doughnuts to celebrate his arrival on the West Coast, Bernie entered the L.A. freeway system. Girlie was whistling and wheezing like the Grand Ole Opry, but he had to keep up. The one time he let the speedometer drop below sixty, a giant set of razor-sharp teeth showed up in his rearview mirror. Some big-rig driver's idea of a joke, a radiator decoration, but it scared the life out of Bernie just the same. "Sorry, Girlie," he said, and kept the pedal to the metal.

He gassed up in Castaic, bought a bag of oranges straight from the tree in Ventura. And then, when he'd begun to believe it might only be a fiction, there was the Pacific. It wasn't blue like in the postcard Winifred had sent him, but the sun sparkled on it just the same. There were even some surfers riding the waves.

California. Bernie could hardly believe his luck. Girlie hadn't made a sound except for good ones since Castaic, even though he'd given her only the low-grade gas. Then, climbing a gentle incline into Summerland, Girlie began to knock. Bernie steered into the slow lane. *Less than twenty miles to go, Girlie. Don't let me down.*

She limped through Santa Barbara. Just as the sun plunked into the ocean and the sky turned to fire Bernie spotted the sign for the University of California. He took the curving off-ramp, his entire body lighter, as if it were filled with a zillion fireflies.

Then Girlie just stopped. One minute she was knocking away, the next she was dead quiet. Bernie coasted down a road that led to a beach parking lot. He could see the lights of a restaurant in the distance, a couple of cars parked near it. He turned off the ignition, though it no longer mattered, and got out. "Good girl," he said, patting Girlie's hood. But it was too late. She'd given up on him. Like Winifred, she'd had enough.

Bernie took off his sneakers and crossed the sand to the edge of the water. Then he rolled up his jeans and let the waves wash over his dirty feet. He stretched his tired back.

Near the restaurant, a wooden pier stretched out into an inky sea. It was hard, seeing that pier, not to think of Gatsby and his famous green light. Bernie didn't want to compare himself to Gatsby, who had been so tragically deceived by the woman he loved. But Daisy was a flighty, shallow thing and Gatsby so dense. No wonder.

He spent what he figured would be his last night in Girlie's bed, staring up at the full moon until his eyes would no longer stay open. The last thing he heard was a girl's hysterical laughter.

A group of children woke him up. They were yelling, chasing each other and a curly little dog round and round in circles on the sand. Bernie changed into a clean T-shirt, ran his fingers through his hair. He ate his last doughnut, grabbed his sleeping bag and his duffel. He put on his windbreaker. The university wasn't far. From where he stood he could see a tower, a tall white tower just like in Camelot.

# NINE

Having peeled off his jacket and dying from heat exhaustion, Bernie trudged down the freeway off-ramp toward the campus. There wasn't a grand entrance or anything, just a parking kiosk and, beyond that, a massive stucco building under construction. CALIFORNIA NANO-SYSTEMS INSTITUTE said the gold letters in a long span over green-tinted windows. Nanoscience, there it was. The phantom enemy that had stolen Winifred's heart.

At the kiosk Bernie got a campus map and located the student dorms. University Road was clogged with cement mixers and backhoes. The whole place seemed to be under construction. Herds of students on skateboards and bicycles cruised through it unflustered. Near some brown brick buildings, several riders stopped and dismounted, locking their bikes in a bike parking lot. Bernie followed them down a sidewalk, into the heart of dormitory central: a hive of multistory buildings placed at odd angles as if they meant for you to get lost. The place was mostly empty, quiet. A groundskeeper walked slowly along the sidewalk pushing an edge trimmer. Then two girls came out a glass door laughing. One slapped the other on the arm. "You're not!" she said. A couple of crows hopped ahead of Bernie, like in a Disney movie, showing him the way.

Bernie swallowed a lump of panic. There must be a thousand rooms here! How would he ever spot the one person he so desperately needed to see that even his eyes were starved for her. He chose a building at random—Anacapa Hall—and walked down the first-floor hallway. The doors were all closed, some of them decorated. Some had names, none of them Winifred's. He went out the door on the other side of the building. It was just possible he'd run smack into her. That's how it happened in movies anyway.

Where the dorms ended Bernie found the University Center. It was the color of a ripe peach and crawling with students. He set his duffel and sleeping bag on a low wall and sat beside them. Already he felt defeated. The place was immense and he'd only seen one small piece of it. Students went by endlessly as if on parade. Finally, he stood and tapped one, a girl, on the shoulder. "Excuse me."

Swirl of dark shiny hair like in that other shampoo commercial. The girl looked up, and up, at Bernie looming over her. "Yes?"

"I'm, uh, looking for a friend but I lost her address. Is there, like, an address book or something for this place?"

The girl's eyes slid quickly from Bernie's face to his sleeping bag and duffel. "Can't help you. Sorry," she said, and hurried on. He tried a couple more students, but they acted as if they all belonged to some secret club to which he would never be invited.

Bernie picked up his stuff and joined the parade going wherever. It didn't much matter where, though he kept his eyes peeled for a mess of frizzy red hair, his ears tuned for Winifred's low-pitched giggle.

One sidewalk took him to Marine Science Institute, a long, low building at the edge of the beach. Bernie walked out onto the sand and looked back toward the beach parking lot where he'd left Girlie. He hoped she'd be okay there until he could get her towed somewhere and have her repaired. But that would take more money than he had left.

He trekked back into the center of campus and bought a slice of pizza from a cart, took it to a patch of grass, and gobbled it in four bites. Winifred was bound to see him eventually. He'd heard somewhere that if you were lost, it was best to stay put and eventually somebody would find you. But if somebody wasn't looking for you, what then?

He got up and wandered some more. The campus was huge, the buildings all different. On a whim, he opened a door to a lecture hall filled with students and slipped into a seat in the back row. The professor, a short balding man in a plaid shirt and jeans, had written PLATE TECTONICS on the white board. As he lectured, the students around Bernie were scribbling madly in notebooks. Without meaning to, Bernie's mind got snagged—this wasn't high school. This was *real*. He stayed until the class ended.

By late afternoon, Bernie was tired of wandering the campus and getting dirty looks. There had to be a better way to find Winifred.

The idea came as he sat on the library steps sipping a cup of coffee. He tossed his empty cup into a trash can and went inside.

Every terminal was busy. Bernie joined one of the lines. By the time he got a machine, his fingers were shaking. He opened the UCSB Web site, tried every link, but got nowhere. He resorted to Google.

Winifred Alice Owens, he typed into the search space, then Owens, Winifred. After several dead ends, up popped a solid purple screen. Neon-yellow fireworks began shooting up from below, while above, a banner of pink names swam in from the left: Calista Bearden, Tory Castagnola, Sam Gray, Wini Owens. Y'all Come Up and See Us Sometime. San Marcos Hall. 6C, the HOT FLOOR!

Wini Owens? His Winifred?

Bernie stared as the letters swam in one side and out the other. A tap on his shoulder brought him out of his trance. The girl waiting behind Bernie asked if he was through. He quickly exited the purple horror and stumbled out of the library into the blinding sunshine.

What had Winifred gotten herself into? The "hot

floor"? There must be another Winifred Owens. He stumbled back into the library, stood in the line, and this time typed in Winifred Owens. Up popped the purple screen. What was Winifred thinking? This wasn't safe! Anybody with half a brain and a computer could find Winifred Owens on the "hot floor" at UCSB.

Fueled by anger and confusion, Bernie made his way back to the hive and at last found the dorm called San Marcos. He looked up at the sixth floor expecting . . . *what*? Flames? But it looked no different from all the others.

Inside the building, he stood in another empty hallway facing the scratched metal doors of an elevator. This was it: the time of reckoning, the moment of truth, the end of the line or a whole new beginning.

He wasn't ready.

Gasping for air, Bernie pushed his way out through the glass doors and began running. Three laps around San Marcos muttering to himself like a lunatic, he was back facing the same elevator doors. He pushed the UP button as if it might bite. The doors parted. Out came a girl wearing a backpack and the face of Greek tragedy.

Bernie got in, took a deep breath, and pushed the button for the sixth floor. The butterflies in his empty stomach were going nuts. Winifred would have to talk to him, at least that. After all this time. After all those years together, she couldn't just close the door in his face.

Could she?

The elevator jolted to a stop on the sixth floor and the doors slid open. Another empty hallway full of closed doors. Was there a message in all this? A Gwen Stefani song bled from one of the rooms. Somebody (boy? girl?) laughed, once, like a bark.

The door marked 6A was covered with photos of kids making stupid faces. There were several pictures of girls in bikinis covered with what looked like shaving cream. One showed a guy on all fours licking the shaving cream off a girl's leg. *Whipped* cream then.

The door to 6B was unadorned, but 6C was a purple and pink Mardi Gras scene with blown-up photocopies of four girls' faces. One had Winifred's nose and round face, but her hair was black.

Bernie knocked softly. No answer. He knocked again, this time with more authority. He listened. Nothing. Kneeling, he rummaged through his duffel for a pen to write a note, then changed his mind. He had to see the surprise on Winifred's face, the look in her eyes when she opened the door. A nanosecond later she'd be in his arms, he was forty percent sure of it. And then? Well, he'd worry about all that when he had her back.

Light-headed, Bernie fled the building. He'd come back later when Winifred returned from class. Maybe he'd buy her a bunch of flowers. Somewhere. Pick them? Two guys bearing surfboards walked past. They were shirtless and deeply tanned, the muscles in their backs shifting as they walked. With nothing better to do, Bernie followed them.

The beach was strewn with strange podlike things on vines. Exhausted, he lay down on a clear patch of sand using his duffel for a pillow. Overhead, a squadron of seagulls sailed past a flat blue sky. Bernie closed his eyes. When he opened them again he was blind. He sat straight up and rubbed his eyes. Beach. Night. Cold sand. He remembered. But it was so dark, the only sound the shushing of waves as they reached for his sneakered feet. Bernie stood and brushed himself off. Hollow of stomach, mind, and soul, he trudged up the beach toward the twinkle of lights in the distance.

# TEN

Rested (sort of) and determined (very), Bernie faced the purple door once again. He knocked.

"It's open!" sang a familiar voice.

Bernie's heart stopped, flipped once, and restarted. He turned the knob and opened the door to a walk-in closet. Or so it appeared. Clothes were strewn everywhere, piled on beds, slung over chairs; shoes with six-inch heels or blocks of wood to balance on were scattered across the floor. A girl with black hair and low-slung jeans was rummaging through a dresser.

"Uh, hello?"

The girl turned, her heavily mascaraed eyes widened, then blinked like a pair of tarantulas doing push-ups. Then, as if in a soap opera, her hand (with nails that were long and polished) went straight to her throat. "Bernie?" squeaked the voice.

For a second, peeking through a painted mask, Bernie thought he saw Winifred.

"Bernie! What are you doing here?"

"Winifred? Is that you?"

Winifred laughed, the old sandpapery chuckle he loved. "Of course it's me. Who did you think it was?"

Bernie's knees turned to water. He sat down on the edge of a chair piled with sweaters. "But you're . . . you're so"—he decided to be kind—"*different*."

"You like?" she said, and did a clumsy little pirouette. Like a silly goose of a girl.

*Winifred.* Bernie couldn't believe it. He was dreaming. He had to be. He'd gone to sleep on the beach and—

The door swung open. And there was a tall blond girl posed in the doorway, hands on half-bare hips. "Wini! You're not ready yet, girl?"

Winifred was frozen, caught between her two worlds. And then, as if apologizing for spilling something smelly on the floor, she turned to Bernie and said, "Calista, this is Bernie."

Bernie had never gotten used to the eye-sweep. High school girls were so cruelly good at it, but this girl, Calista, was a true master of the art. Her eyelashes barely twitched, but he knew he'd been had.

"Nice ta meetcha," she said, dismissing him. "Are you coming, Wini?"

"I, uh . . ." Winifred looked from Calista to Bernie and back to Calista. Bernie almost felt sorry for her. Almost. "Well, Bernie just got here, and . . ." She frowned at Bernie, as if it was he who had made the mess on the floor. "Bernie, what are you *doing* here?"

With a practiced toss of her head, Calista threw back her hair. "Okay, well, look. Here's the deal." She sighed through her nose. "Come when you can. Bring Bertie if you want."

"Bernie," said Bernie.

Calista frowned, as if she'd missed an easy answer on a multiple-choice exam.

Winifred's smile was shaky. "Okay, sure. Right. Bernie can come," she said doubtfully.

When Calista was gone, the air seemed to leak right out of Winifred. She fell backward onto a bed, throwing an arm over her eyes. Bernie studied her bloody-red toenails like they held some sort of code until she sat up again. "Bernie," she said. Then she gave a helpless shrug and began to cry. Little chuffing sounds, her face buried in her hands. After a while, she looked at him. With an angry swipe, she smeared black tears across her face. "Darn you, Bernie!"

Bernie crossed the room and sat beside Winifred. He carefully took her hand with its frightening nails. "I had to come, Winifred," he said. "I needed to see you. I was *dying*."

"Oh, Bernie," she said. She blew her nose in a towel.

What emerged to look at him with wide sad eyes, and a more or less clean face, was almost his Winifred.

" 'Oh, Bernie' what?"

"Things are different now. It's not . . . I'm not . . . We're not . . ." She searched the ceiling but whatever she was looking for wasn't there.

"Not *what*?" Under Bernie's feet the floor began to have a quicksand feel to it. "I love you, Winifred. I always have."

She gave him a lopsided grin.

Bernie leaped to his feet. "No! I mean it. Winifred! I've missed you so much. My life . . ." Bernie threw up his hands. "It *sucks* without you in it."

"Poor Bernie," said Winifred, shaking her head.

"I don't want your pity, damn it! I want . . . Oh, Winifred. I want *you*! I want *us*!"

Winifred looked at Bernie so seriously that it nearly tore him apart.

"Come here," he said, holding out his hands. She let him pull her up. He gathered her into his arms. Her hair felt like plastic. She laid her head against his chest and, in what felt to him like surrender, put her arms around his waist. "All I've thought about, all I've dreamed about is us," he said with a cracking voice. Winifred looked up and when she did, Bernie was ready. His mouth swooped down and caught hers in the middle of saying his name. The hairs from Bernie's toes to the ones on his head stood at attention and cheered.

Both hands flat against his chest, Winifred shoved Bernie so hard he stumbled back against a desk. "Stop it!" she said.

"What? Stop what?" He was hanging from a cliff here, shivering in a hailstorm. The crocodiles were snapping at his feet. What was she saying?

Winifred crossed her arms over her chest, which, now that Bernie thought about it, had somehow gotten *inflated*. "Things change, Bernie. People change."

"Not me," he said miserably.

"Well," said Winifred in a voice that seemed to belong to somebody else. Calista? Bernie wondered. "Maybe that's the problem."

The door burst open again. "We brought the party home!" cried a pencil-thin dark-haired girl, producing a bottle of wine from under her UCSB sweatshirt. In seconds flat the room was filled with a dozen bodies. Somebody switched on some music and the walls began to thump.

"Winifred?" called Bernie, but she had been swallowed by the crowd. A girl with the biggest boobs Bernie had ever been near began bumping her butt against his thigh. This, Bernie understood, was a signal to dance, but his feet wouldn't move. "I'm Tory," said the girl, who was really sort of beautiful in a big-chested way. "Are you a Sig?"

"Do I have a cig?"

"No, silly," she yelled, "Sigma Alpha Nu! The frat house."

"Oh," said Bernie. His feet were shuffling now in what could pass for dancing. "Sigma nu to you, too."

At last he got a chance to dance with Winifred, and for the length of one song he was happy. Then she was gone again.

When the first bottle (and then any bottle) came his way, Bernie took a swig. He began to feel lighter, then incredibly wiser. Taller by half a foot than anybody in the room, he gazed down Gulliver-like upon the Lilliputians. They were a silly lot, these college kids. They screamed and carried on like four-year-olds at Chuck E. Cheese. He danced easily now, energetically, with whoever came his way, and sometimes by himself. He kept one eye on Winifred, who was making a big point of ignoring him. For one whole long Eminem thing, she was dancing with a guy they called Rob. Rob looked like somebody, some movie actor, and Winifred was star-gazing up at him while he scoped out all the other girls. Bernie wanted to wipe the floor with this guy. Who did he think he was anyway?

But the alcohol was busy convincing Bernie that he was the better person, more mature, an actual man. He danced away, getting into the beat now, stepping on somebody's foot. His head began to spin. Where was Winifred? (*Who* was Winifred?) He stopped dancing and made his way— *Excuse me, Pardon me, Oops, sorry!*—through the sweaty, writhing bodies, the laughing, screaming mouths, toward what he hoped was a bathroom. Occupied. Sounds of agonized retching from within. Bernie slid down and leaned against the wall. When the door opened and a girl stumbled out, Bernie crawled in, shut the door behind him, and, hugging the toilet instead of his Winifred, lost the remains of his lunch.

* * *

Bernie awoke to the ceiling caving in on him. Bump, bump, bump went the ceiling. He opened his eyes, fully alert. A bed, he had gotten himself under a bed. Somehow. But whose? Winifred's? And if it was Winifred's, was it she bumping above him? And if it was she, Winifred, who was she bumping with? Over the sound of the bumping, he could hear the frantic pounding of his own heart. He held his breath and listened harder. *Winifred's* grunts? *Her* panting? How could he tell? They'd never done it, never actually made love. And, anyhow, what was going on up there wasn't love, or at least he didn't think it was. *Urg, oh! Now, now, now. Uh, uh. Yes! Unhh, unhh, unhh.* After a while Bernie put his hands over his ears and just endured it, waited it out. At last the mattress was still. Somebody rolled off the bed. He watched a pair of hairy legs going toward the bathroom. The bathroom door closed. From above came a huge yawn.

Bernie bumped his head on a metal strut. "Winifred?"

The room grew very still. Where did the party go?

"Winifred?"

Reddish-blond hair, then an upside-down freckled face, peered over the edge of the bed. "Who's under there?"

Bernie slid out, skinning his elbow on the bed frame. "Nobody," he said. "I mean, I thought you were my girlfriend." He got to his feet, rubbing his elbow.

"Oh," said the girl, holding the sheet to her neck. "Who's your girlfriend?" She somehow managed to light a cigarette one-handed, shook out the match, and blew a long plume of smoke at the ceiling.

"Winifred Owens," he said. "This is her room."

The girl looked down at the tangled sheets and considered. "Oh. Yeah, well, mine was taken."

"Hey, dude!" A clap on Bernie's shoulder made him wheel around, and there in the buff was Rob.

"Don't mind me," said Bernie. "I was just leaving."

"Good idea, dude," said Rob.

"I'll tell Wini you were looking for her," giggled the girl, "under the bed!"

# ELEVEN

A week of lonely anguish, and Bernie was already becoming somebody he didn't like very much. Like a whipped dog or a cheap detective, he began following Winifred wherever she went. By seven forty-five in the morning, he was sitting in the back row of an old movie theater eating a doughnut, waiting for Winifred and her cohorts to arrive. He'd watch her shiny black head bobbing as she whispered and giggled to Calista or Sam (Tory seemed to be the only one paying attention) and wonder if there was anything left of the mind that used to dazzle him.

Halfway through the lecture he'd leave and slink back to campus. Unlike the soc class, Winifred's English class was small, so he'd wait outside until it ended, watching birds hopping around or the errant cloud cross the sky. In a dusty corner behind a bookshelf on the library's eighth floor Bernie found a place to stash his sleeping bag and duffel. Before the library closed, he'd retrieve them and head for Girlie and a fitful night's sleep. He ate in the UCen cafeteria, choosing things that were cheap but filling.

Another week passed. Almost broke, Bernie couldn't seem to do anything but what he was doing. Watching Winifred. Stalking, he supposed it was. He could tell she knew he was there by the way she carried herself.

One morning on the way to class he got her to talk to him, and the conversation was almost like old times. If you didn't pay attention to the words.

"What happened to nanoscience, Winifred?"

"I prefer Wini now," she said. "Really."

"What happened to nanoscience, Winifred?"

"Oh, *that*," she said, dismissing centuries of hard physics in a sweep of her bloody nails.

With the sheer power of his desire, he forced her eyes to meet his. "Doesn't this remind you of another talk we had once?"

Blank look.

"You and me, only reversed." He mimicked her nagging voice as he remembered it. "What are you going to do with your life, Bernie?"

Winifred made a sour face. "Well, what *are* you going to do with your life, Bernie?"

"Don't you worry about me, *Wini*," he said. "I've got plans."

But he didn't.

Bernie began snatching leftover food from cafeteria

trays, half a sandwich here, the remains of a taco there. It was amazing what the students left behind, enough food for an army. Bernie was simply taking care of what would have been washed down the disposer. Bernie Federman, the human recycler. At first he was sneaky about it, but nobody seemed to notice; or if they did notice, they didn't care.

On a Wednesday at two forty-five, Bernie was sitting in a pool of sunshine on the library lawn when it hit him that he was bored. It was a feeling that made him uncomfortable, an empty, scary feeling, reminding him of the time after his mother died when he and his father had tried to drown themselves in the meaningless drivel of television.

But when he looked up, there was Winifred, head down, walking toward South Hall and her English class. Bernie arose like an eighty-year-old man with arthritis and scuffed along behind her. But when he got to the classroom this time, he went in.

Most of the desks were already filled. After shooting him a sour look, Winifred had taken a seat in the very back row, which would have surprised Bernie once. Thinking about what he might say, what excuse he might give when the professor showed up, Bernie slid into a seat halfway back, slumping down to make himself as small as possible.

"Hey there! Sorry I'm late!"

What Bernie guessed was the professor strode into the

room. Slapping an overstuffed leather briefcase on the desk, she launched into a grisly story about a guy who slept himself to death. It took Bernie a full ten minutes to understand she was talking about a story. She was more like an actor than any teacher he'd ever had, flinging her arms, sighing and laughing, then stopping on a dime to pin somebody in the class with a question.

And tall! Almost as tall as Bernie, or so it appeared from where he sat. Not a whole lot older either, with hair frizzy as Winifred's (before life on the hot floor) in a blond halo around a long, narrow face. Bernie was spellbound, so caught up in the story and her that he found himself sitting up straight.

"And you—" she said, sighting down the gun barrel of her long arm straight at Bernie. "I'm sorry, tell me your name again."

"Bernie," he croaked.

"Loss!" she cried. "What do you make of it? This wife, those children, so suddenly alone?"

Eyes wide with expectation, she held out both hands, like a Baptist preacher, for Bernie to enter the conversational waters.

"I, uh, I dunno," Bernie muttered. But she wouldn't go away.

"You've experienced loss," she crooned. "We all have. It's the human condition! What do we do when faced with such pain?" She was actually leaning over him now, her thin arms anchored to his desk. Her hair smelled spicy. Her eyes were green and blue with flecks of yellow, like mica. She gave off sparks.

"Run?" said Bernie.

Up went her freckled arms. "Exactly! We run. Or we lose ourselves in something, some*body*, anything to try and ease our pain."

She shot Bernie a smile (for being good? for not running?) and turned away. Bernie's heart which had shot into his throat thumped back into his chest and tried to resume its normal dull rhythm. He couldn't take his eyes off her. Diedre, they called her. Not professor, not even Miss or Ms. Just Diedre. She was so alive that Bernie, at last, woke up. His brain, like an atrophied muscle, stretched itself and began to ache.

Instead of following Winifred back to the dorms, Bernie went to the reserve book room at the library. He found the novella called "The Death of Ivan Ilyich" and read it twice. Why, he could write a story like this! The thought was shocking in its way.

He hadn't thought about writing for a long time. What was driving him anyhow? Well, *her*. Diedre. She could make a story seem real, alive, earth-rattling. But it was more than that. For Bernie, it was like standing in a buffet line after a three-day fast or, because he'd never really done that, seeing Winifred again. Literature filled a hollow place so hungry it had forgotten the taste of real food.

* * *

The campus emptied out for Thanksgiving and Winifred disappeared. She wasn't going home, she told him that much. There had been talk of skiing in someplace huge. Mammoth. Maybe the place was called Mammoth. But he was broke and couldn't follow. He spent the long weekend with Girlie.

On the afternoon of Thanksgiving Day, Bernie took the number 24 bus into downtown Santa Barbara. The streets were empty and the shops were closed, which made him feel even lonelier than if he'd stayed on campus. He decided to call his father. The least he could do was to cheer up the old man, who would no doubt be sunk in his memories of Bernie's mother's famous oyster dressing and pumpkin chiffon pie.

"Dad? It's Bernie."

"Hey, son! Great to hear your voice!" In the background Bernie could hear people talking, then a fluttery female giggle.

"I just called to wish you a Happy Thanksgiving."

"Same to you, son. Hey, you should be here! You'll never believe who came into the shop a couple of weeks ago. Beatrice. Remember Bea? Mom's roommate from college?"

"Um, sure. I guess." His brain Googled and came up empty.

"Well, she's on her own, too. Lost her husband in '97."

"That's good. I mean, oh, Beatrice."

"Heck of a good cook, Bernie," his father whispered, like it was a secret. "Best darned turkey I ever . . . Well, outside your mother's, of course. We've got a real crowd here. So! How are you? They cooking you a bird at the college?"

As far as his father knew, Bernie had some sort of arrangement at UCSB where he was taking classes for free. Things were going great with him and Winifred, just as he'd hoped.

"Sure," Bernie said. "Turkey, dressing, cranberry. The whole nine yards." Then he told his father the pickup was still parked at the beach (gathering dust, but so far no citations).

"Sell it," said his father. "It'll only bleed you dry from now on."

*Sell Girlie?*

"You be careful now, son."

"You, too, Dad."

Frowning, Bernie hung up the phone. Did his dad have a girlfriend? A woman friend? An actual woman? In their mother's kitchen? All this time had he only been waiting for Bernie to get a life so that he could get on with his? It didn't seem possible, but there it was. Bernie walked down State Street, trying to scare up a feeling of happiness for his father but succeeding only in feeling sorrier for himself.

And the lower he got, the lower he got. Stopping by the

beach on his way back to campus, Bernie found only an empty parking spot where Girlie used to be.

* * *

Monday morning, the campus was back to normal. Bernie hung around Winifred's room that afternoon reading short stories while Tory did her nails and Winifred read *Allure*. The girls didn't seem to mind that he hung out, not even Winifred, which was a little surprising. There was an air of impending doom now that replaced the pre-Thanksgiving frivolity, though nobody seemed inclined to start studying. Two weeks until final exams, and under all her makeup, Winifred had begun to look green. She'd never flunked an exam, but neither had she tried to learn a whole course's worth of information in a couple of weeks. Plus she had to write a paper for Diedre that was already overdue. Bernie asked her how the paper was going, but she refused to discuss it.

"Are you happy, Winifred?" Bernie had succeeded at last in drawing her out for a walk around the lagoon by telling her she was putting on weight. It was a mean thing to do, but not half so mean as she'd been to him.

She'd let him take her hand, which was a shock. Like the boyfriend and girlfriend they used to be, they walked the path that ran beside the water. Bernie tried hard not to put too much store in this. He knew if they ran into one of the girls (unlikely this far from the center of campus), she'd drop Bernie's hand like a hot rock.

"Am I happy? Of course I'm happy. I'm exhausted I'm so happy."

Bernie ducked to get a good look at her expression. The old Winifred would be joking, but *this* one?

The water in the lagoon was still. Growing along the shore was something Bernie supposed was weeds, though they were kind of pretty for weeds. A pair of ducks paddled past in perfect compatibility, unlike a couple of people Bernie could name.

"Win—" he left it at that. "Is there . . . Do you think there could be a chance, you know, for us? I know things are different. I can see that. But it's still the same old us, isn't it?"

"Is it?" she said, looking up at him. "I don't know, Bernie." She smiled a sad, brave smile. "Sometimes I look at you and suddenly I remember some silly little thing we did. Nobody was as close as us, nobody!" She said this fiercely. Bernie's heart, that waddling duck, lifted and, for a moment, soared free.

"I know! Winifred, I know!"

"But other times, I look out and see this whole other life where I'm not tied to anybody. Where nobody tells me what to think or do." Winifred dropped his hand. "Maybe if you had a little respect for what I'm trying to do, there *would* be a chance. To be friends, at least."

The duck landed with a thud. "But what are you trying to do, Winifred? Really, I'm just trying to understand."

She turned and faced him, fists on her hips. "It isn't easy learning to be your own person, Bernie. You should try it sometime."

"Your own person? Winifred?" And then he was spouting again, waving his arms like a person about to drown. "You're Calista! You do exactly what everybody else does. You say the same stupid things, wear the same stupid clothes. You gossip!" He saved the most damning piece for last: "Winifred! You're a *communications* major!"

Winifred stopped, her glossy watermelon-colored lips pinched. "Thank you very much, Bernie Federman, for your enlightened view of my character." She sniffed. "And now you can take your opinion and shove it you know where!" Chin up, Winifred clunked off on her four-inch platform sandals. Bernie thought about going after her, but what would he do then? Apologize? For telling her what she needed to know? For telling her the truth?

# TWELVE

In English class, Bernie's hand went up like a jack-in-the-box, like Winifred's used to. It wasn't only to impress Diedre. This was for him, to people the deserted tenement that had once been a thriving, active brain.

On Wednesday of Dead Week, Diedre called to him as he was leaving class. Bernie froze in his tracks. She was onto him. She'd found out he was an impostor. She'd probably call security.

He turned to face his fate.

"I don't think you're officially enrolled, Bernie," she said, eye to eye. He had her by an inch, maybe. "Do I even have any grades for you?" She reached toward her roll book.

"Well," he said, sorting through several fabrications. "I'm not. Enrolled. Actually, that is."

She cocked her head. There were exactly six freckles across the bridge of her nose. One front tooth was trying to push the other aside. She wasn't pretty, not by a long shot, but something about her was *electric*.

"You're not enrolled? Why do you come then? I'm curious. This is a required course. Nobody takes it by choice."

Bernie would have faced a firing squad before admitting the truth: he was a stalker, a fool, a guy in love with a princess who turned out to be a frog. "I like what we do in here. I like writing," he said. "I always have."

"Oh, so you're auditing then."

"Right!" said Bernie. Auditing? Was that like borrowing?

Diedre bit her lip, evaluating him, it seemed, looking at him in a way he'd never been looked at before. It made him blush.

"So you're not a freshman."

"No." That, at least, was the truth.

"I didn't think so. A senior then. Students mature so much between their freshman and senior year." She gathered up her notes, stuffed the textbook into her briefcase.

Bernie the senior cleared his throat. "Uh, would you like to get a cup of coffee or something?" He tapped his foot nervously. Asking the professor out for a sort of . . . *date*? Had he totally lost his mind?

When she smiled, one side of her mouth went up more than the other. Her naked lips reminded him of Winifred's, the way they used to be. "Sure," she said. "Only I'm buying. I'm just a TA but I know how broke you students can be."

Well, you could only wash a shirt so many times before it began to shred. Anywhere else but on a college campus, Bernie would be taken for one of the homeless. Which he was. As the weather grew cooler, Bernie had taken to bedding down behind a bookcase in the library. Nobody seemed to need the information on the eighth floor: Ancient Babylonian Law, the Agrarian History of Macedonia. Even the custodians had deserted the place, leaving dust bunnies to multiply in corners, and cobwebs to stretch themselves across shelves of unloved books. As long as Bernie didn't leave the building during the night and set off the alarm, he was fine. Warm. Comfortable enough.

The old Winifred would have loved the adventure of it.

Diedre took Bernie to the faculty club for coffee. The lounge had floor-to-ceiling windows that looked out upon the lagoon, ruffled by an onshore breeze. Identical fat little brown birds raced along the water's edge.

Diedre was "mired," she said, "bogged down" in finishing her dissertation and revising her novel (she'd written a *novel*!). It was nice to get her head out of the books for a little while and relax. They sat together on an ancient leather couch sipping coffee out of real cups with saucers. There were important-looking paintings on the wall. So civilized, so *grownup*. Once, in the middle of the conversation, laughing, she touched his knee, lightly, with the tips of her unpolished fingernails. Bernie jumped. He almost levitated. She didn't seem to notice.

She asked him all sorts of questions about himself. At first, he was cautious. Before answering, his brain raced: What would a senior think? What would a twenty-two-year-old college student say? But after a while, he relaxed. And then—how did it happen?—he was telling Diedre all about his mother, and then about Winifred and her pursuit of nanoscience that had devolved so quickly into fashion magazines and frat parties.

She smiled softly, shook her head, or nodded in all the right places. What an amazing listener she was! How was it he'd decided she wasn't pretty? She was gorgeous.

"You have a first-rate mind, Bernie," she said, when at last he wound down. "People shy away from writing not because they hate it—which is what they'll tell you—but because they can't understand it. It's language at its most difficult and sometimes most frustrating. It can bring a . . . a *nanoscientist* to his knees."

Bernie's laugh was almost hysterical. He'd slept so fitfully in Girlie or on the library floor, eaten so poorly that he'd lost ten pounds. Sometimes, like an addict in need of a fix, his hands shook. And here was this . . . this *woman*! Sort of, well, *flirting* with him.

Or maybe not flirting, actually, but interested, definitely interested.

"Well," she said, setting her empty cup on the sideboard. "I'd better get back."

Stalking had become so much a habit that Bernie could

easily have followed Diedre home. Instead, as they parted outside the faculty club, he asked her where he could get a copy of the book they used for class. "Like cheap," he said. "Free would be best."

She reached into her briefcase. "Here," she said, and handed him her copy. "It's marked up, but it's yours if you want it."

"You're kidding!"

"I don't kid," she said. "It's a shortcoming."

He watched her cross the bike paths toward Isla Vista, the adjoining community where many of the grad students lived. She leaned a little to the left, her briefcase like an anchor weighing her right side down.

Bernie practically ran to the library. In class, he'd gotten an idea for a paper, something to do with transformation and the soul's dark night. It was brilliant, or would be. He'd write it for her, for Diedre, to justify all the great things she'd said about his intelligence. (Well, just that one thing, but that was enough to fuel ten papers!) He worked until the library closed, then made his way up to the eighth floor, where he slept like a baby.

# THIRTEEN

The truth, when Wini let herself face it, was that she wasn't really all that happy. But why exactly was that? She was living the freshman dream. She had friends, a wildly busy life—three or four parties a week, fabulous shopping excursions, trips to all the hot L.A. clubs. She could now choose a top for any outfit just like *that*, without a second thought; do the three-color eye makeup thing in her sleep. Like an overstuffed pillow, she was filled with self-confidence, positively bursting with it.

Even her parents were excited for her. Well, they hadn't seen her grades yet. But she could explain those. College grades were so much lower than high school grades. You had to adjust your expectations, her father had warned her. Fortunately, she'd had the good sense to drop calculus before midterms and consider a different major. Communications made so much more sense than a science. Why, there were *dozens* of careers you could choose from after graduation.

The life she and Bernie used to talk about? How silly was *that*? Teaching English in Africa? Finding a cure for AIDS? Saving the rain forest?

Well, they were kids. You had to grow up and get real. Media, that's where the action was. Anchorperson at a major news station would be a dream job.

That's what Rob said leaving soc last Wednesday. The whole anchorperson idea began with him, actually. "You've got the kind of face people trust," he'd told her. "You know, like Katie Couric."

Rob was so amazing. He'd walk into a party, a class-room, even a giant lecture hall, and the place would practically ignite. He was going into politics after graduation. Only he was going to be more careful than his father, a state senator, who was under indictment for something, he couldn't remember what. Some meaningless thing.

Thoughts of Rob were seeping into Wini's mind, though she really didn't have a chance with him. He'd been Calista's boyfriend in high school, then Sam's for a while in October. After that he began playing the field. Like a soccer goalie, his hands and arms went everywhere.

They saw the way she looked at him, her wise roomies, and they tried to warn her away. "He's not for you, Wini," Calista said, in an uncharacteristic show of genuine concern. "He takes what he wants. You understand? And then he takes off. He's missing, like, a part or something."

"Yeah," said Sam. "A heart. He's the Tin Man."

But Wini wasn't alone in her desire for Rob. Tory had designs on him as well. He just happened to fit all her specifications for the college man she intended to land: he was rich, gorgeous, athletic, and taller than she was in heels. But he wouldn't get around to asking her out (or agreeing to meet somewhere, which, if you stretched things a little, you could call a date).

"He knows you're a virgin, Tor," Sam said. "It's not like he has a conscience or anything, he just doesn't like to fight for it."

Tory wasn't taking their advice either. "Is sex all you two ever think about?" she said. "If a guy can get all the milk he needs, he isn't exactly going to buy the cow, you know."

"Bull," said Sam.

"No, really," said Tory, frowning. "It's the cows that give the milk."

"I thought they all did," said Calista.

"You're kidding, right?" said Wini. Could you actually get into college without knowing where milk came from?

Wini began to construct a whole new theory. Rob was smart, really smart. He didn't even have to study. The reason he didn't stick with any girl for long was obvious: they bored him. Calista and Sam were fun girls, but their minds were blank books. Calista actually thought the Secretary of the Interior was in charge of decorating the White House. Whenever she, Wini, got a chance to talk about real stuff with Rob—some theory about the divergent conversational patterns of men and women, say—he'd hang on her every word.

Not for too long, but the potential was definitely there. Tory was her only real competition.

Bernie was driving her crazy. Nothing Wini could do or say would change his mind: she and he belonged together and that was that. The girls all thought he was cute, in a lost-puppy kind of way. They didn't know how smart Bernie really was. But once in a while he'd surprise them all by bringing up something they were supposed to have learned in soc. Like that socialization stuff about how anybody could get sucked up into one big group mind if they weren't careful. Bernie looked straight at her while explaining all this (he'd actually been reading the textbook). So she could tell he really didn't understand what was going on with her, how she was growing as a person and becoming herself. How could he be so blind?

Dead Week, the week before finals when studying got serious, ended with the usual Friday night blowout. Wini spent the better part of an hour perfecting her look, trying on a dozen different outfits and checking with the girls. She didn't tell them about her secret mission: tonight Rob was going to wake up and realize Wini was more than just a brain. She'd ask him out if she had to. Girls did that sometimes. Well, the unpopular ones did. But really, when you thought about it, who decided that boys should do all the asking out anyway? Society, that's who. The group minds. A girl who was trying to be her own person wouldn't let society tell her what to do, would she?

She hoped Bernie wouldn't party with them tonight. He

was still such a geek. The way he danced? His arms flopping around like that? She almost couldn't watch. It made her shudder to think she'd danced that way once. And it was positively scary to think how easily she'd fallen back into that rhythm with him when they danced close together his first night here. For the length of a song, she practically lost herself to Bernie again. Why was that? She didn't even love him anymore.

Well, she cared about him. How could she not after all those years growing up together? It was a brother-sister thing, that's all. She simply had to ignore the feelings her body got when she danced with him, or during those times she let him hold her hand. It was probably some kind of body memory, a leftover thing. Her body didn't know how uncool Bernie was. He wasn't even *trying* to change, or to make anything of himself. He just hung out, like a ghost, a poor, lost spirit. He'd actually said in front of everybody that the anchorperson thing was "candy." "Where's your social conscience, Winifred?" he'd said. "Or did you lose that, too?"

"Too?" What was that supposed to mean?

The party was on the third floor of a condemned apartment building on Del Playa. It was practically tumbling over the edge of a cliff, but what a view! Wini and Sam hit the keg for cups of foamy beer and went out to the balcony. Calista and Tory had disappeared somewhere. Sam was waiting for a guy named Carlos that she'd met in her media class. Meanwhile she seemed willing enough to gaze at the full moon with Wini.

So Wini confided her plan.

"Oh, hon, it's too late," said Sam. "Rob and Tory—" She touched Wini's arm. "Don't look now, but they're right behind us. You knew she had the hots for him, Wini." Her dark eyes grew wide and tragic. "Oh, Wini. I'm so sorry."

Wini's throat had a lump in it she couldn't talk over. She clutched the rail like she was riding the balcony straight into the sea.

"How could I be such a moron?" she said, when she could manage to talk again. "I could just shoot myself! I thought maybe he, you know, *liked* me. I mean, sometimes the way he looks . . ." She quickly swiped away a tear.

Sam found a tissue in her bag. Wini dabbed it carefully under her eyes. "He's like that, Wini," Sam said. "We told you. It's just Tory's turn, that's all. Just when she starts to think she's nailed him, he'll do this trick mirror thing and disappear. You'll see."

"Oh, poor Tory," said Wini, forgetting not to turn around. And there was poor Tory dancing with Rob behind the glass, dancing boob-smashingly close while a reflection of the crescent moon shimmered over their heads. It was exactly like in some glossy magazine ad for diamonds ("Give her the world and she's yours"), it was that romantic. Hard as it was to feel sorry for Tory, Wini tried.

"Come on," said Sam, taking Wini's hand. "Let's go see if Carlos is here yet. Maybe he brought a friend."

# FOURTEEN

Bernie knew about the party on Del Playa. It wasn't exactly a secret. Part of him went into what had become automatic: he got ready to go.

In a letter addressed to him in care of Winifred, Bernie's father had sent him a check. He said he didn't want Bernie to work so hard that he didn't have time to study. Bernie tried to remember what he'd told his father about finding a job. What lie he'd told. What had become of him? Bernie the stalker, Bernie the scavenger, Bernie the liar. He bought underwear and an olive-green T-shirt at Kmart, saving the rest to buy a real meal now and then.

The automatic Bernie grabbed his plastic bag of toiletries, his new shirt, and underwear and headed over to the gym. But after his shower a very odd thing happened. Combing his hair at the mirror, thinking about Diedre, a wiser Bernie began gradually to emerge from the steam. Instead of going to another stupid party to spy on Winifred, he went back to the library.

By ten o'clock closing time, Bernie had printed out all fourteen pages of his paper, "The Soul's Dark Night: A Quasi-theoretical Investigation of the Images in 'The Story of an Hour.'" He stood and stretched, filled with something he couldn't at first identify. Joy? Pride? Life? All three? He couldn't wait to show the paper to Diedre.

Maybe he didn't have to wait. In the phone book he found a listing by last name and first initial that could only be hers. With shaky fingers he lifted the receiver and called her.

She was glad to hear from him, she said. Why didn't he just come over? She'd gotten some good work done, too. They could share a bottle of wine she'd been saving for a special occasion. But life was short, right?

Passing San Marcos Hall, Bernie looked up at the sixth floor without the usual pang of loneliness. Was he getting cured? Was it possible that there was life beyond Winifred?

Diedre lived in an apartment above Morninglory Music and up a flight of rickety steps attached to the back. A pot of something dead sat on the landing. When Diedre came to the door, Bernie took a step backward. "Wow," he said. "You look great."

"Thanks," she said. "Come on in." When she turned, the golden dragon on the back of her black kimono shimmied. In bare feet, she padded across a tiny book-filled room and snuggled into a corner of a futon. "Sit," she said, patting the space beside her.

There were candles everywhere. That spicy smell again—perfume? incense? her?—permeated the room and made Bernie light-headed.

"So," she said, "tell me about your paper."

"It's right here," Bernie said, reaching for his backpack.

She stopped his hand. "Later," she said. "Just tell me about it."

He watched her pour two glasses of purplish red wine, with hands that looked so . . . *naked*. His mind kept spinning around this really dumb idea, that she had nothing on under that kimono. Her feet and legs were bare, and the kimono kept sort of slipping where her breasts were. Bernie pulled his mind back from that dangerous (but thrilling) precipice and, with a shaking hand, took the glass she handed him.

The wine was thick and dusty-tasting and went straight to his head. Diedre was watching him with this look on her face, in her eyes, that he couldn't describe if he tried.

It was intense though, really intense.

Now that he was here, he felt sort of silly about his paper. He was really just a kid, and here was this . . . this *woman*. This grown woman who was looking at him like . . . Well, maybe he *could* describe it. She was looking at him like a jungle cat stalking its prey on the Discovery channel.

She was looking at Bernie like she wanted to eat him.

He hopped up and excused himself.

"Down the hall to your right," she said. As he left the room, he could feel her eyes on his back.

At the mirror in the closet-sized bathroom, Bernie planted his hands on the edge of the sink and stared into his own eyes. It was time to take the big step. Time to be a man. This was serious. She probably thought he had plenty of experience, when all he had were a bunch of frantic make-out sessions with Winifred.

So okay. Time to make a move. What was he doing hanging around in the bathroom? What was stopping him?

Winifred. There she was in the deep pool of his eyes, where she'd been since he was fourteen. He felt like an about-to-be-unfaithful husband who'd just slipped off his wedding ring.

But this was crazy! Winifred didn't love him anymore. Bernie was free. Free to have sex, the actual thing, with a real woman, an almost-professor.

He took a quick sniff of his armpits, regretting that he'd put the $2.99 stick of Right Guard back on the drugstore shelf. Carefully, he inched open the medicine cabinet. Dry Idea, that would have to do. It was unscented, so she'd never know.

Diedre hadn't moved from her spot on the futon. Bernie sat and took a gulp from the glass that was full again. He wanted to tell Diedre how beautiful her eyes looked in the candlelight, all sparkly and golden, but how corny was *that*?

Well, the thing about women was you didn't know what you should do or say at any given time. He'd been on pretty solid ground with Winifred, and then look what happened. She'd turned into a whole other person practically before his eyes. And now this *woman*, who'd recharged his dead brain cells like a twelve-volt battery, had transformed herself into a stalking cat. What was a guy to do?

But he didn't have to think very hard about it. "You want to kiss me, don't you, Bernie?" she said sort of lazily, leaning back against some soft-looking pillows. "You want to kiss me real bad."

Bernie gulped. "I do? I mean, yeah, I do!" He lunged toward her.

"Hey, slow down!" she said, laughing. "Take it easy."

"Oh, yeah. Um, sure."

The shock of Diedre's lips, of a foreign tongue, different spit! Bernie pulled back. What was he expecting? But he knew. Diedre was so not Winifred that even his dumb body, which, if truth be told, would have gone for anything with breasts, shrank back into itself. Of course he had to go on kissing Diedre. What else could he do? He didn't want to hurt her feelings. And anyhow, it got better. But when she suggested they pull out the futon and get comfortable, Bernie hesitated a second too long.

"We're moving too fast, aren't we?" she said. "You're

right." She gave him a peck on the lips and stood. "I've got some cheese and crackers and stuff. Why don't you turn on a light? You can read me your paper."

Bernie watched Diedre bend to reach into a small refrigerator while his body morphed itself back into dullness. How was it that a person could be so relieved and so disappointed, both at the same time?

She set a plate of cheese and crackers on the coffee table. "So," she said, folding her hands like a sermon was about to begin, "let's hear it."

Bernie's stomach fell. Which was worse? Having to prove his manhood or putting his flaccid mind to the ultimate test?

He cleared his throat and began to read, "Since the beginning of time, when man began to write on cave—"

"You can skip the intro," she said. "Start with the next paragraph."

"Huh? Oh, yeah. Okay."

He'd struggled for an hour and a half over that intro! What was wrong with it? Launching into the second paragraph, a sort of extended introduction, Bernie heard his voice begin to climb. His palms broke out in a sweat. He was twelve again. Diedre sighed, but Bernie plowed on, determined to show her . . . *what*? What did he have in mind for this paper anyway? The thesis seemed to be missing. His voice droned on and on. The Dry Idea wasn't living up to its name. A candle flickered once and died. The floor lamp shining on him made him feel like he was being interrogated in the room with the one-way mirror on *Law and Order*.

The ending was good, he was pretty confident about that. As he read it, his voice deepened and steadied. The last line was a real clincher: "In the inevitable maelstrom of potent anxiety, one feels the pangs . . ." The final sentence had dropped into his lap, just like that, from a muse or something. It made his spine tingle.

Silence. Bernie looked up from his paper. Diedre's multicolored eyes were gazing steadily at his face. "Nice job," she said.

His voice hit another high note. "You like it?"

"Well, it's rough. A draft. But, yes, it has an original quality about it I seldom see."

Original. He'd take that for a good thing.

"Strike the first page—"

"But—"

"—and the conclusion."

"No!" yelped Bernie.

Diedre smiled. Then she frowned. "Well, of course, it's your paper," she said. "It isn't like I have to give you a grade or anything, since you're not enrolled."

"I don't care about a grade," Bernie said, reeling as if he'd been punched in the gut.

"Good!" she said. "That's refreshing."

"I like to write," he said.

"You like to write."

"Yeah! I do. I really do."

"What about it do you like?" She yawned without making any attempt to hide it.

"I don't know," he said, but he really did when he thought about it. "I like to put words together," he said. "I like the way they almost, I don't know, *gather* themselves, like magic. The way they can be like good music. I like trying different combinations, different sounds. I know I'm not great at it. Yet."

"No?" She was smiling now, awake.

"But the work is fun. It's actually fun. It sure isn't changing tires."

"That's wonderful," Diedre said. She reached up and pushed the hair back from his face. "How old are you, Bernie?"

Bernie grew hot. All over. He gulped. "Old enough," he said, looking as steadily as he could into her eyes.

Diedre said nothing for what seemed like eons. Then, with a smile Bernie couldn't read, she laid her hand firmly on his thigh. "Good," she said, "because I'm going to *so* enjoy being your teacher."

# FIFTEEN

Finals arrived. The students who had kept up were in a state of mild panic.

The girls in 6C were frantic.

Calista called for a mandatory study session. Snacks were bought, along with caffeinated drinks. It was time to get serious. Bernie watched all this from a corner where he was sitting on the floor reading the last chapter of Wini's soc text.

"So. Okay. Who's got notes?" Calista was sitting like the Buddha on her bed. While the others cleaned the room, she had changed her toenail polish from Melon of Troy to Wanted Red or Alive, and now she was ready to study.

"Not me," said Sam in an offhand way.

"I've only got the first four lectures," said Wini guiltily, flipping open her notebook.

"Tory?" said Calista.

Tory came back from space. "Unh-uh."

"Well, that's just great," said Calista. "Doesn't anybody remember anything?"

No one replied.

"What's there to remember?" said Bernie from his corner. "It's pretty obvious stuff."

They all turned to look at Bernie. "You took notes?" Calista asked incredulously, as if Bernie had no hands.

Bernie shrugged. "No. But I listened. And the textbook is pretty straightforward."

"Oh, sure," said Sam, rolling her eyes. "Like it's easy."

"Well, it's not rocket science," said Bernie. "Take chapter one, for example. Social Construction. Pretty straightforward, like I said. It's the way we create our selves, what we're going to become. We're influenced by everybody around us, of course. Parents, teachers, mostly our peers." He stopped, a silly grin on his face, as if he'd made a joke that nobody caught. He went from Social Construction straight into the Looking Glass Theory.

Calista and Sam were spellbound. Even Tory, who'd been sleeping way too much, was sitting up straight. Wini felt like a mother listening to her brilliant son explaining the theory of the universe, she was that proud.

Bernie seemed different somehow, more relaxed, sort of . . . *centered*. Now that Wini thought about it, Bernie hadn't been around for days. She hadn't seen him at the last party either. As Bernie launched into the final chapter, Wini felt the first pull of something unraveling. Could it be that Bernie was finally giving up?

And wasn't that exactly what she wanted?

"Well, I can't believe it!" said Sam when Bernie was gone. ("Gotta meet somebody," he'd said. "See ya.")

"You didn't tell us he was a brain!" said Calista accusingly.

Wini smiled like the Cheshire cat. For the first time, she was sitting atop the 6C heap. Maybe she wasn't as pretty as Calista or Sam, maybe her boobs weren't *there* like Tory's, but she had the smartest boyfriend.

Well, *friend*. She had the smartest friend. It wasn't the coup it seemed at first, but it was something.

On Wednesday morning, Wini looked up from her English text at nine-twenty and saw that Tory was still asleep, rolled up like a burrito with a blanket over her head. She went back to the short story she was reading for the first time, but couldn't stay focused. Something was wrong with Tory. She was sleeping too much and not eating. She'd cut several classes. As a friend, it was up to Wini to get her to talk, especially since Calista and Sam were unconcerned.

Wini made up her mind. If Tory was still sleeping when she returned from class, well then she'd just have to wake her up.

But then this strange thing happened. Wini had decided to sign up for one of Diedre's extra study sessions. Adding her name to the list on the desk after class, she looked up and saw that Bernie had stayed behind as well. And that he'd had his hair cut.

He actually looked, well, sort of *cute*.

"Thanks for helping us with the soc, Bernie," said Wini wholeheartedly. "We might have a chance to pass the final, and only because of you."

"No problem," he said.

"No problem?"

He shrugged. "Right, no problem. Happy to help."

Was he teasing? Bernie hated that expression. How many times had she left a store with him waving his arms and spouting about not having *intended* to cause a problem in the first place?

Calista said "no problem" all the time. Was that Bernie's point? Wini used to be able to read Bernie's mind, but for some reason it was getting harder to do.

Wini glanced at Diedre, who was going over a story with one of the girls in the class. Then she went ahead and did what she'd only half a mind to do before. She smiled up at Bernie and said, "You know, there's this really cool place in town called Quantum. We could go there for dinner. My treat. You know, to pay you back."

"All of us? Or you and me?"

"Whatever," she said.

"Whatever." He shook his head sadly. Sad because he

wanted a real date, or sad because she'd used another over-used expression, Wini wasn't sure.

"Well, do you want to? You and me? If you don't want to—"

"No, it's great. Sure. When?"

"Friday? That's the night before I leave for home." Even a dinner date with Bernie would be better than going date-less to the last big party of the quarter, the post-finals blowout. "Quantum?"

"Is that a restaurant?"

"Sure, silly. Meet you at the bus circle at seven-thirty."

Her feelings tossed like confetti, Wini left the class-room. She got all the way down the hall and out the building before she realized she'd left her backpack on her desk. She turned and went back to the classroom, opened the door, and there was Bernie. With Diedre. At least it looked that way, like they were, well, *together*. Diedre had her hand on Bernie, actually touching his chest. And they were standing so close. When the door opened, both their heads turned. Bernie took a step back and Diedre's hand fell away. "Wini?" he said.

"I, uh, forgot my backpack," squeaked Wini. She scur-ried like a gopher to the back of the room, grabbed her pack, and scurried out again.

Bernie? Diedre? Could it be? It couldn't be. Diedre was old. Well, a heck of a lot older than they were. Six years at least.

Wini found herself practically racing back to the dorms. Maybe it wasn't what she thought. Diedre was the touchy type, that's all. But touching his chest? That didn't seem right. And Bernie didn't exactly look unhappy about it. The thing was, Bernie was so *innocent*. He hadn't learned the moves of the singles scene. Girls could be so calculating when it came to boys, so predatory! And Diedre was a bonafide grownup woman. At dinner on Friday, Wini would have to have a heart-to-heart talk with Bernie. Who better to do it than she?

Which made her remember her promise about Tory. Well, here she was turning into a regular counselor. Probably due to her interest in communications. Already she was putting her intended major to good use.

But it was hard to erase that picture from her mind, Bernie and Diedre looking so . . . so cozy.

# SIXTEEN

Wini poked at the burrito and it stirred. A corner of the blanket came down. "Whah?" said Tory, one eye open.

"Sit up, Tory," said Wini.

Tory pushed herself up on her palms and leaned against the wall. Her hair looked like she'd been in a wind tunnel. "What's wrong?" she said blearily.

"That's what I want to know," said Wini. "You're sleeping all the time, for one thing. You didn't even go to your media final."

Tory frowned. "What day is it?"

"Wednesday."

"Oh, crap," said Tory. "It was this morning."

"What's going on?" Wini said. "Calista says it's PMS, but it's not. Is it? It's Rob."

Tory pushed the blankets back and slid her legs off the

bed. She stood, crossed the room, went into the bathroom, and closed the door.

What would a counselor do now? Wait, she supposed. Be patient.

The toilet flushed and Tory came out. "When's the soc final?"

"At four," said Wini. "Want to grab a cup of coffee? Get some lunch or something?"

Tory climbed back in bed and pulled the blanket over her head.

"Tory?" Wini stared at the blanket-wrapped figure of her roommate wondering what she should do. She couldn't handle this alone. Where were Calista and Sam?

At Nicoletti's probably, having a nonfat cappuccino. Wini headed for the UCen. On the way, she considered unloading her concerns about Bernie on the girls. Well, of course she would. They'd assure her that she was imagining things, and then she'd feel much better.

But nobody she knew was at Nicoletti's. There were kids everywhere, sharing tables, studying or sleeping on couches and chairs, a veritable sea of strangers. All at once a scary feeling descended on Wini like a huge black bag: she didn't know anybody. Not the way you were supposed to, like, *know* people. Tory hadn't confided in Wini as she'd expected, as she herself would have confided in any of them, as a true friend. And Calista? Sam? Did she really even know *them*? Come to think of it, which she really didn't want to do, what did their conversations amount to anyway? Just a bunch of gossip? Was Bernie right after all?

Suddenly, she needed to talk with Bernie, the way they used to, sitting on his front porch or walking through the zoo. He would help her sort through all this stuff, analyze it like a chem equation. But where could she find *him*? He slept in the library, she'd heard, on one of the upper floors. There were other rumors about him, too, that he ate leftover food and stole clothes out of the Salvation Army donation box. After all he'd done, even crossed the country for her! Why hadn't she extended a hand in simple friendship? Given him some money? He'd never borrowed a dime from her in the past, but clearly he'd lost his pride. He'd been going straight downhill, her friend Bernie, and there she'd been all this time . . . just *gossiping*.

\* \* \*

Wini searched the sixth floor and then the seventh floor of the library for signs of Bernie. She was about to leave the eighth floor when she spied something green poking out from behind one of the short bookcases. Was it the tail of his green stocking cap? It was! He'd brought it all the way from home.

And there was Bernie's lair. A plaid blanket had been laid on top of his sleeping bag, as if he'd actually made up a bed. Next to the "bed" was a stack of books, on the top of which was perched the little-bitty silver book light she'd given him last Christmas, when he'd given her the half-heart on a gold chain to wear around her neck. It didn't go with everything now that she knew how to dress, so she never wore it anymore. But Bernie still wore his. At least he was wearing it the day he'd tutored them in soc.

Wini tried to remember if he had the half-heart on today. He didn't! It would have been right where Diedre had laid her hand. She looked down at the sad little camp Bernie had made for himself. No wonder he'd let Diedre maul him. He was dying from a simple lack of human affection.

Wini's eyes filled with tears. Poor Bernie! An upscale dinner was the least she could do for him, the *least*. As the elevator descended, Wini blew her nose. Peering into the smeared image of her face in the stainless steel door, she reapplied her lip gloss. Maybe Calista and Sam were back in the room by now. And if Tory was still asleep, well then they'd all confront her together.

But Tory wasn't in bed. Tory's bed had been stripped. Wini checked out the bathroom. "Tory?"

Wini sat on the thin, lumpy mattress, her mind racing. Where was Tory? She stood and pulled open the top drawer of Tory's dresser. Empty. All the drawers were empty. Her computer was gone.

Wini dialed Calista's cell.

"Gone?" said Calista. "What do you mean she's gone?"

"Her stuff," sobbed Wini. "There's nothing here. No

shoes under the bed. That shampoo she won't let us borrow, you know, the imported French stuff? It's not in the bathroom!"

Calista swore. "We'll be right there. Look in the closet. If her leather jacket's gone, so is she."

Wini hung up and searched through the clothes stuffed into the closet. No brown leather jacket, the one Tory's father sent to her during one of his business trips in Spain.

Wini expected Calista and Sam to come bursting into the room any minute. Half an hour later, she heard a single note of Calista's laughter from down the hall. The girls came in carrying coffee to-go cups.

"See, the thing is," Sam was saying, "he's not all that hot. He just *looks* hot, you know what I mean?"

Calista nodded sagely. "I know exactly what you mean."

Sam dropped her purse and backpack on Tory's mattress. "This is so weird," she said. "Are you sure Tory didn't leave a note or anything?"

"I looked everywhere," said Wini.

"Well, she didn't say anything to me," said Calista with a shrug.

"Which she would if anything was really wrong," added Sam.

"I think she's depressed," suggested Wini.

Calista frowned. "Tory? Depressed? Nah."

"Maybe not," said Wini. "But don't you think it's weird she never told us anything about her date with Rob?"

Calista and Sam did an eyelock. "Wini's right. She never said a word."

Post-date wrap-up. Wini had been in on all the sessions, even though she hadn't had a real date to analyze. If Dating 101 were a course, they'd all be getting straight A's in it.

Sam bit her lip. "What time did she come in that night?"

"I dunno," said Calista.

"It must have been really late," said Sam.

"Or really early," said Wini.

Calista dialed Tory's cell, which hadn't even occurred to Wini.

"Tory, it's Calista. Where are you? Call me."

Wini suggested they try Tory's number at home. Calista, obviously put upon, sighed and looked up Tory's home phone number. She plunked down on Tory's bed.

"Mrs. Castagnola? Hi!" Calista's voice had turned to butter. "Tory said something about going home this weekend. Did she get there yet?" (She held her palm over the receiver and hissed at the girls: "Taking a shower.") "She is? Oh, great! Right. Sure. Well, right. That's true." She rolled her eyes. "Would you tell her to call us? Thanks, Mrs. Castagnola!"

"Well, that's a relief!" said Sam.

"She could have left a note!" grumbled Calista.

"I don't think she took all her finals, you guys," said Wini. "She could flunk out. Something's happened to Tory."

* * *

It was Friday evening and Wini was sorting through her clothes, trying to decide what to wear for her dinner with Bernie. Since it was Quantum, the L.A. look was practically required. But that meant sexy, and she didn't want to give Bernie the wrong idea. Anyway, he'd just wear that ugly green T-shirt and his ratty shredded jeans. They'd probably get a table way in the back next to the restrooms, like they had in Pittstown the night before she left for California.

Tory hadn't returned Calista's call. Sam decided that one of them had said something, not intentionally, of course, but that Tory had taken it the wrong way. When she came back to campus, they would all sit right down and talk about it. They'd simply have to learn to communicate better. After all, wasn't that what communications majors did?

With Calista's help, Wini settled on a pink pleated miniskirt and a simple white angora sweater. Going out with Bernie had at least this going for it: she could wear her highest heels, the ones she couldn't walk in that well.

Winifred applied a third and final coat of mascara. It was almost time to meet Bernie at the bus circle. Calista and Sam were in the bathroom doing their makeup together. She called goodbye but they didn't hear her.

And who should she practically run right into in the hall but Rob! He was wearing a pale blue shirt, silk it looked like, and a pair of soft-looking gray slacks. Actual slacks. There were comb marks in his hair, as if he'd come straight from the shower. His cologne smelled extra expensive.

"Heading for Del Playa?" he said. "Where's the rest of the gang?"

"They're coming," she said. Wini's heels brought her eye-level with the dimple in Rob's chin. His skin was smooth as a girl's, but somehow that didn't make him less sexy.

"Leave 'em," he said, with a nod toward the elevator. "Let's you and me go."

"You?" she squeaked. "Me?"

"Yeah. Hey, you're looking really hot, Wini." His slow once-over made Wini shiver.

"Cold?" he said, and slipped his arm around her. They walked down the hall like, well, exactly like it was a date.

They were sailing down El Colegio Road in Rob's black BMW before Wini remembered Bernie.

Well, that wasn't *exactly* true. She'd thought about Bernie going down in the elevator, walking out to Rob's car parked illegally at the curb. She thought about Bernie when she slipped into the BMW's black leather passenger seat that was curved like a palm. And she went anyway.

Wini kept trying to breathe right. Everything was in soft focus—oncoming headlights, Rob's profile, the little numbers on the speedometer—as if she'd had a sudden loss of vision. She blinked and looked out the side window at the weed lot used for rugby games.

At the light Rob made a left turn and headed toward Del Playa, where Wini knew all the end-of-finals parties would be happening. Too bad her roomies wouldn't be there to see her when she walked in with the catch of the day, of the quarter. And maybe even beyond the quarter, who could tell?

"How did finals go?" Rob said. "I'll bet you aced them all, am I right?"

The truth was too dismal for Wini to think about. If she ended up with C's, she'd be lucky. But Rob had aced his for sure.

"I thought they'd be harder," she said, with, she hoped, the right note of nonchalance.

"I should have studied more," Rob said, careening around a girl on a bicycle. "I've *got* to get myself off AP."

"Advanced Placement?"

Rob laughed. "That's high school, Wini. I'm talking about Academic Probation. You know, when your grades drop too low. I partied a little too hearty last term. Now I've got to pull up the old GPA or—" Rob drew a finger across his throat.

"Or what?" said Wini, alarmed.

"They kick your butt out! What did you think?"

Wini felt a little sick, like she'd eaten something rotten for dinner, when she really hadn't eaten a thing since lunch. "They just kick you out?"

"Hey! Not to worry, Wini. You aced your finals."

"Uh, maybe not," said Wini.

He leaned over and slapped her thigh. "Well, it's too late to worry about it now. It's time to party!"

They turned onto Del Playa and started cruising for a parking space. Screeching to a stop, Rob backed expertly into a tight spot.

"I don't know about you," he said, "but I'm ready to get bombed!"

Wini bit her bottom lip. Was Rob serious? Was this what he called a date?

But it wasn't a date. He hadn't asked her out. He'd picked her up. There was a difference. The date she had, or was supposed to have had, was with Bernie.

Wini blinked away the thought of Bernie waiting at the bus circle, sitting the way Bernie sat with his long arms draped down between his knees.

Rob got out of the car and began walking toward the apartment building. All the lights were on and Wini could hear the distant thumping of music, like jungle drums.

"Coming?" Rob said, turning back toward the car at the last minute, as if he'd already almost forgotten she was there.

# SEVENTEEN

Bernie waited, hunched on the bus circle bench, arms dangling between his knees. After weeks that seemed like months, like an ice age, Winifred was finally coming around. Bernie could hardly believe it.

Poor Winifred! The look on her face when she'd burst into the classroom and seen him with Diedre. He couldn't have planned that if he'd tried. Bernie's loud guffaw surprised a woman waiting at the other side of the circle. "Another nut," her look said.

Diedre had taken the blame when Winifred, with an expression of pure panic, fled the room. "I should be more careful," she'd said. "There is a faculty code of conduct, you know, that I'm supposed to pay attention to. But, Bernie?" she shook her head. "You're just so different from all the other students. I forget sometimes you're not in grad school. What are you doing Friday night? There's this concert you'd love at Soho. Shall we go together?"

"Great," he'd said. "But wait. What does it cost to get in?"

"Five bucks. Don't worry about it."

Later that afternoon, feeling guilty for having put it off until practically the last minute, Bernie had left a folded note on Diedre's office door saying that something had come up. He couldn't go to the concert with her after all.

Scribbling the note, Bernie knew he should be calling Diedre instead, leaving a live message at least. Diedre wouldn't find the note until Monday. It was a wimpy way out.

The bell in the tower chimed eight times. Winifred was late. No surprise, at least not for the way she was now. It took her an hour to get ready to go anywhere. He hoped she wouldn't wear all that makeup tonight.

Well, of course she would. The more face goop she plastered on, the less she looked like Winifred, and the more she became Wini. Maybe she would always be Wini.

Then what? The thought that scared Bernie most was the one he kept pushing from his mind. For not quite four and a half years, he'd been in love with Winifred, centered his life and planned his future around her. He'd seen himself over and over again mirrored in her eyes exactly as he wanted to be. That's what true love did for you. But was he in love with *Wini*? And if not, what then? What did his life mean?

A scarier thought yet, who *was* Bernie Federman?

Maybe he should have gone to the concert with Diedre after all. She, at least, seemed to have some idea of his worth, or at least his potential. Or he should have stayed "home."

Written something brilliant. Started his novel, maybe. When he was writing, he knew who he was, or at least who he would become.

Three buses arrived and departed. Passengers got off and others got on. He watched a young couple snuggle down into a seat on the number 24. The girl looked at the boy so tenderly that Bernie had to turn away.

He leaped to his feet and looked across the dark stretch of campus toward the dorms. Better walking than waiting. He'd meet Winifred between here and there probably, all flustered because now, for some stupid reason, they were going to be late and lose their reservation.

But when Bernie knocked on the purple door, nobody answered. He stood there for a minute more, revisiting the four girls' faces, remembering how he'd thought none was Winifred's. What a shock it had been to see her again! And here he was, still hanging around, holding out hope that things would somehow get back to the way they used to be.

Wasn't this what crazy people did? Obsess like this? Go over and over the same old ground? Maybe somewhere along the way he really had lost his mind. How did you know that anyway? If you were crazy, how did you know you were crazy?

Bernie rode the elevator down and headed back to the bus circle. Winifred had stood him up. He couldn't believe it. But he'd bet his last dollar that he knew just where she was.

He stuck his hands in the pockets of his windbreaker and, head down, began striding angrily toward Isla Vista. He didn't care who Winifred was with at the party, or how deeply he would embarrass her. He was going to tell her exactly what kind of a person she had become: thoughtless, shallow, a ditz in hundred-dollar jeans. And he wasn't going to the airport tomorrow to say goodbye either. As he strode, he composed a brilliant speech in his mind. "This is goodbye, Winifred," he'd tell her at the end of it. "I never thought I'd say it. Have a good life. Or at least a *real* life."

Then, before she could stop him, he'd turn away. Walk off into the sunset. Well, into the dark. There wasn't any moon to speak of.

The party in the wrecked apartment on Del Playa was in full swing. Bernie scanned the crowd, but didn't see Winifred. He didn't see anybody he knew. Then, when the kitchen door swung open, he caught a glimpse of Sam. He dodged through the crowd and pushed his way into the kitchen. Sam and Calista turned, stopped in the middle of side-splitting laughter.

"Bernie!" Sam said, widening her eyes at Calista.

"Where's Winifred?" Bernie asked, tight-lipped.

"Well, she *said*," Calista said, "she had a date with you, but then—"

"Calista!" warned Sam.

"What?" said Bernie. "But then what?"

Calista rolled her eyes. "Well, okay, she was here with . . ." She flicked her hand dismissively and walked away.

Sam put her hand on Bernie's arm and for a moment Bernie saw the real person she might be. "She was with Rob, Bernie. But they're not here now."

"Rob? She's with Rob?" Bernie swallowed down what felt like shards of glass. He turned and slammed through the swinging door.

Rob? *"Good idea, dude!"* That Rob? Winifred wouldn't stoop that low, would she? Couldn't she see what kind of jerk Rob was? Did she think a guy like that could be trusted?

She probably did.

She *did*. Winifred trusted everybody. And besides, what experience did she have with guys? None. Zilch. Zero. He, Bernie Federman, was her only experience. The nice guy who never pushed her any further than she wanted to go. The guy who walked off a hundred hard-ons just to keep a stupid promise. For what? So that some horny frat boy could have her? For all he knew, it could be happening right now. He groaned.

Outside, Bernie slid down against the building and sat with his head in his hands. It was over. Whatever deep, unbreakable bond he thought he had with Winifred was as fictional as the novel he would one day write.

Winifred in the moonlight, Winifred's beautiful, practically untouched, absolutely unviolated white body in the moonlight. The thought of that creep's hands on his Winifred—

"Bernie?"

He looked up. Sam.

"I think I know where she is," said Sam. She held out her hand to help Bernie up. "The frat house. His. Sigma Alpha Nu, the one at the end of El Sueno. Or Cordova. I think El Sueno. I can find it."

"Well, let's go then!" he said, grabbing her hand. "Take off those stupid shoes, if you have to."

Sam kicked off her strappy heels and hid them under a bush. "Manolo Blahniks," she said wistfully. "I hope they're still here when I get back."

"Screw Manolo what's-his-name!" cried Bernie. "Run!"

# EIGHTEEN

Running wasn't exactly Bernie's strong suit, but he did his best to keep up with Sam, his nearly worn-through sneakers slapping the concrete sidewalks. After several wrong turns, Sam at last pointed to a nondescript three-story apartment building. It was one of those buildings that looked threatening in a very quiet way. SIGMA ALPHA U said the letters over the door, the N gone missing. A few of the windows had slits of dim light leaking through closed blinds, the rest were dark.

Pumped with macho courage, Bernie crashed through the front door (which, unlocked, could easily have been opened).

The foyer and front room were dark.

"Winifred!"

"Dude!" said a voice. "Keep it down."

As his eyes accustomed themselves to the dark, Bernie saw that there were conjoined bodies in several places—

couches, chairs, on the floor. Muted jazz. A thick smell hung in the air. Alcohol, cigarette smoke, feet.

"Winifred!" Bernie shouted.

"Rob?" Sam called in the direction of the stairs. "Are you up there?"

"In his room," mumbled a voice. "Third floor."

"*Which* room?" said Bernie.

"It's the one at the end of the hall," Sam said, but Bernie was already bolting up the stairs three at a time.

Knives were stabbing his oxygen-depleted lungs. When he reached the third floor he leaned over, gulping air. Then he exploded into action, pounding on every door, yelling Winifred's name.

A head popped out of the third door. "What the hell?"

Bernie went for the head and it popped back inside.

"That's not his room," Sam gasped, dragging herself up the last couple of steps. "Last door."

"Winifred!" yelled Bernie. "Winifred, where are you?"

At the last door Bernie made a grab for the knob just as the door opened, and, like an actor in a bad play, out stepped Rob.

"Dude! What are you doing here?"

Bernie tried to push Rob aside. Rob wasn't budging. Bernie stuck his head into the dark room. "Winifred?"

"Dude. You're interrupting a man at work here. Why don't you and—hey, *Sam*! I didn't recognize you under all that sweat!"

Sam stuck her hands on her hips. For a second, at least to Bernie, she looked just like Wonder Woman. "Rob, is Wini with you?"

Rob frowned, or leered, Bernie couldn't tell which. "Who's Wini?"

"You creep! You jerk! You flaming two-bit—" Bernie leaped at Rob. Rob too easily pushed him aside. Bernie got into a boxer's stance and raised his fists. Rob jumped right into Bernie's arms, knocking him off his feet. They rolled together on the floor, flinging off-center punches, pulling hair, and screaming like girls in a catfight. It was nothing like Bernie imagined a fight to be, but in a senseless, painful way, it felt good. They rolled and swore, and finally staggered like drunks to their feet, holding each other up. Then Rob grabbed Bernie around the neck and tried to bend him over. Bernie elbowed Rob in the ribs. For a couple of seconds they were apart, breathing hard, blood everywhere, on the walls, smeared all over both of them. A crowd had gathered without Bernie even knowing it. They were cheering, some of them for him. He pulled back, fist ready to plow right into Rob's arrogant little nose, when the lights went out.

\* \* \*

Bernie blinked up at the circle of unfamiliar faces. "It's your nose, dude!" said the owner of one of them. "Old Rob got you good."

"Yeah," said another admiringly. "I think it's broken."

Somebody tossed Bernie a moldy-smelling gym towel.

Bernie reached up and tentatively touched his nose. Still there, though it felt like it had been chewed on by wolves. Blood dripped steadily down both sides of his face into his ears. He sat up. Dizzy, he laid his forehead on his knees.

"Better get that beak looked at, dude," said a voice behind Bernie as he limped down the stairs and out the door.

It had started to rain. The cool air began to clear his head. Holding the towel under his nose to stanch the blood, Bernie made his way toward the end of the campus where he remembered seeing the Student Health building. He hoped they wouldn't ask for his student ID. What could he be but a student? Who else would be stupid enough to mess himself up like this over a girl?

Over a lost cause. The truth of that hit Bernie like the fist he hadn't seen coming. It was over. Winifred had made an ass of him. She'd stood him up for someone else. She had gone to another guy's bedroom. She'd probably had the Big Moment with someone else, a jerk, a frat head, somebody who didn't even know her name.

He laughed bitterly, remembering his and Winifred's vow to save the Big Moment for their wedding night. How many times had he and she, fumbling, breathless, gone to the absolute edge and somehow stopped? How many times had he been driven, yes *driven*, to the point of madness—because it was so very clear to him now that it had all been *her* idea, the wedding night thing—and been turned away at the very portal of fulfillment?

And to think he could have done it with Diedre! Six or seven times by now! But no! He had wanted his first time, his first actual time to be with Winifred.

Conveniently forgetting how frightened and intimidated he'd been by Diedre, Bernie marched toward the bright white lights of Student Health.

Closed. It figured.

Where to go? The library was closed, too. Everything was closed. And Girlie was gone, towed, probably sold for scrap metal.

Heck, the way he treated her, Girlie was probably glad to go.

Bernie huddled in the corner of the library's portico, beating himself up all over again. What an idiot he'd been, throwing his whole life at a silly girl who didn't even want him. Who would want him anyway? He was homeless, friendless, brainless, living in poverty, and soaking wet. No good to himself or anybody else.

Worse, he was talking to himself. He'd hit bottom.

After a while, Bernie calmed down and began watching the rain, how it made everything gleam silver. He'd write that. Tomorrow, first thing. It almost made him feel better.

# NINETEEN

Wini pretended to be sleeping when she heard Calista yawn and roll out of bed. Bare feet slapped the tile floor, the bathroom door closed. The shower started with a rusty squeal Wini had long ago grown used to. Sam was on her back, snoring.

These morning sounds were as familiar as those she grew up with, her mother's wheezing espresso machine, the newspaper landing on the front steps. Living with three girls had become so quickly intimate. How fast she'd given herself over. But wasn't that understandable? She'd never had a sister, and suddenly she had three. Three girls who were, each in her own way, so much wiser in the ways of the world than she.

All her life, she'd only had one real friend, a guy.

But it wasn't Bernie's fault that she'd had no other friends. Bernie hadn't made her (socially constructed her!) into anything she wasn't already. They were kindred spirits when they met in middle school, and, with the ideas and opinions they thought were so original, so brilliant, kindred spirits they remained.

They had been naïve, that's all. Not that original or brilliant, as it turned out. Just different from most. The world was a much bigger place than it looked to be from Pittstown, New Jersey. Wini hadn't been ready for it. Hadn't been brave enough to walk into this room, this hothouse, day after day and be her quirky, unfashionable, different self.

She had caved without a fight.

Sam's feet hit the floor. "Wini? You awake?"

Wini didn't answer.

Last night's "date" with Rob had been a disaster. She'd followed him inside and watched him disappear into the crowd. Soon he was dancing with Keisha, a knockout African American girl from 6E. Wini had counted to one hundred. Twice. Why, she didn't know. Then she escaped into the bathroom. When she came out, Rob and Keisha were out on the balcony. Without a word to anyone, Wini left.

A half-dozen times on her way back to campus, inventing the most sizzling lines to stab Rob with, Wini had gotten lost. For several blocks a friendly dog followed her, a big red mutt with jowls and sad wet eyes, but then he, too, deserted her.

She desperately wanted to call Bernie. If only they hadn't made that ridiculous cell phone agreement.

If only she hadn't been such a fool.

She heard Calista come out of the bathroom and Sam

go in. Wini feigned sleep. How could she tell them about last night? How could she stand their sympathetic sighs or, worse, their I-told-you-so's? At last, both girls were gone and Wini got up.

She began packing her suitcase, sorting through the clothes (why on earth had she bought this awful purple sequined thing?) her parents had never seen. What would they think, her unpredictable mother especially? Would she smile indulgently or frown at all the bad taste? Her father would no doubt ignore the fact that Wini was no longer a redhead. He wouldn't want to deal with it, with what her black hair might mean.

Here was something to think about: how much makeup would she wear on her two-week break? Who was taking the two-forty-five flight out of Santa Barbara anyway, Winifred or Wini?

The girls had planned to meet at Nicoletti's for a farewell cappuccino and Christmas gift exchange at eleven. Instead, Winifred set her present for Calista (the new Madonna CD) on her desk and Sam's (cranberry body glitter) on hers and scribbled them a note.

> *Girlz:*
> *I'm going to try to catch an earlier flight.*
> *Have a great Christmas break! See you*
> *next year.*
> *Wini*

She anchored the note with the cranberry glitter and headed to the shower. If she hurried, she'd have the rest of the morning to spend with Bernie.

* * *

Bernie sat at a table at the Santa Barbara IHOP with a big white bandage on his nose. The doctor at the rapid care center who had patched him up and given him a prescription for pain also gave him a warning: "There are better ways of solving problems, young man," he said. "Better yet, ditch the girl."

A copy of the *Santa Barbara News Press* had been left on Bernie's table. Scarfing down banana pancakes smothered in raspberry syrup the color of clotted blood, Bernie searched the want ads. There was a job in a tire shop, but he couldn't bring himself to circle it. He never wanted to change another tire in his life, unless it was his own.

At the end of the column of part-time jobs, which he checked next, was an ad offering a room and a small salary in exchange for dog care (he had experience!) and gardening. He circled it and finished his breakfast.

From the pay phone, Bernie dialed the number in the ad. He arranged to meet a Mrs. Calendar at her home at eleven. It was twenty minutes after nine.

When the shops opened, Bernie began looking for a Christmas present for his father. He didn't think he had to buy one for Beatrice. With the check his father had sent for Christmas, Bernie could have gone home, but he wasn't ready for that yet. The plans he'd begun making were too new, and possibly fragile. Going home might put an end to them. There, he'd resign himself to working in the tire shop. He'd take the easy way out.

Here, he would be challenged. He was going to have to find out once and for all (if anybody ever did that) who he was. What he was made of. A test of character, he guessed it was. One of those things that got magically worked out in movies over a short weekend, or in the final chapter of a novel, but that, in real life, was bound to be tough.

For sure, it wouldn't be as easy as changing tires.

\* \* \*

Eloise Calendar lived in a ramshackle cottage surrounded by McMansions in the city's Riviera district. Bernie knocked on a blue door that had a wreath made of dried flowers on it.

"Oh!" said the round, gray-haired lady who answered. "Are you Bernie Federman?"

"Yes, ma'am."

"What happened to your nose, son?" She reached out as if to touch it and Bernie flinched.

"Wrecked my truck," he said. It was the first thing he could think of.

She hired him immediately, whether because she was sorry he'd wrecked his car (and his nose) or because she couldn't get anybody else, Bernie didn't know. And didn't care. He felt bad starting off again under false pretenses. But it was much easier to claim he'd been in a car wreck than a life wreck.

He followed Eloise Calendar through the house, which he could have done with his eyes closed since they moved so slowly. She never stopped talking. Every picture on the wall, every piece of furniture or ceramic doggy knickknack seemed to have a story begging to be told. By the time she took him up a flight of stairs behind the garage and showed him his room, it was after noon.

The room was more than he could have hoped for. Against one whitewashed wall was a narrow single bed with a faded plaid bedspread, next to it a yellow wooden chair like one he'd seen once in a Van Gogh print. Under the single window, sunlight flooded down upon a small wooden desk. It was an actual writer's retreat.

The dogs, Silkies she called them, were all at the doggy beauty parlor. All? How many could there be? Bernie didn't ask. He'd find out soon enough.

"I'll take you through the gardens on Saturday morning," she said. "Meanwhile, if you need anything just open the window and yell."

When she was gone, Bernie carried the yellow chair over to the desk. He sat down on it and gazed around his new room. Then, like Goldilocks, he went over to the bed and sat on it, too. Perfect. A real bed. He couldn't remember when he'd last had a good night's sleep.

Winifred was going home today. He didn't know what time. For all he knew, she was at the airport right now. The old Bernie would have taken the earliest bus to the airport and waited around all day if he had to, just to say goodbye.

Instead, the new Bernie took the bus back to campus. He collected his things on the library's eighth floor and made the return trip to Santa Barbara. By three, when Winifred's plane was winging its way across the country, Bernie had settled in and hung a small, framed picture on the wall.

The cracked and faded photograph was of an old man with a pointed white beard. He was sitting at a rolltop desk on which there was an inkpot, a quill pen, and several books. The man was looking out the window—you couldn't see the window but there was light shining on his face—and wore an expression that had stopped Bernie dead in his aimless wandering through the flea market. It was hard to tell exactly what the old man would say if Bernie could, like, *channel* him, but it was clear that he'd lived a rich, full life, a life in which he'd made a profound difference in the lives of people, and all because he'd chosen the way of the writer.

"Yoo-hoo!"

Bernie went to the window. Eloise Calendar waved up at him. "Come down!" she called. "Come meet my little darlings."

They were anything but. Spoiled brats was more like it. Bernie's first job was walking six little dust mops that each went in a different direction, crossing leashes, gagging as their rhinestone-encrusted collars pulled them back. It was hard enough just keeping their names straight: Penelope, Portia, Peterkin . . . He forgot the rest, except that they all began, for some reason, with the letter *P*.

On Friday, the last day before the city college break, Bernie picked up an application, along with information on scholarships. Tuition was unbelievably cheap, but not for an out-of-state student. He'd have to find a second job. He salivated over the writing courses in the spring schedule of classes.

He explored the campus. From a perfectly manicured lawn, he looked out to the ocean where the whitecaps danced. A cool wind ruffled his hair. Like the old Ford pickup resurrected by his father, Bernie felt himself starting up all over again. He might not be much in the beauty department, but what did that matter?

# TWENTY

One look at Wini made her mother swoon. But she revived when Wini asked to be whisked off to the salon, where her black hair was restored to its original color, more or less, only with a better hairstyle. A shopping trip was offered and turned down. Wini dug through an old trunk for the clothes she'd left behind, a pair of flannel-lined "fatty-pants" jeans, a worn-soft Princeton sweatshirt, sweatpants, and a favorite ratty sweater with holes in the elbows. In the bottom of the trunk she found her olive-green hat with the pom-pom and a pair of shredded Converse sneakers. She put the shoes on and laced them up.

When Bernie hadn't magically shown up at the airport, Wini was devastated. And so her return trip was much like the one that brought her to UCSB: a series of stops in restrooms to weep and blow her nose. She had been so confident that Bernie would forgive her. He always had. Bernie was kind and good and promised he'd always love her. But like everything else, love changed. Wini hadn't counted on that.

Wini's love for Bernie had been like her childhood love of Santa or the Easter Bunny: absolute, passionate, and, as far as little Winifred knew, infinite. She had never forgotten how it felt that Christmas morning when she was seven to peek over the stair railing and see her mother laying all the Christmas presents under the tree, while her father munched on Santa's cookies and drank all his milk.

That was the feeling she carried with her through her days at home, the feeling that, for better or worse, it was time to grow up.

Still, it was nice to be home. Nice to sleep in her own bed. Nice to spend time with her parents, who surprisingly, once she looked like her old self again, treated her like an adult. What would they have thought if they could have followed her around one wild weekend at school? It made her feel small. She read her soc text, all of it, even the parts that required a second or third reading. The short stories she'd skimmed, she now read slowly, trying to recall what Diedre had said about them. Then, giving up, tried to make sense of them on her own. She remembered how embarrassed she had been whenever Bernie raised his hand in class. She'd wondered at the time why Diedre's eyes seemed to wander his way. And now she knew.

Was Bernie with Diedre now? Wini's mind fought to erase a dreadful X-rated picture of Diedre and Bernie making love. Diedre, being older, would of course know everything. She would show Bernie the moves, and Wini would sink to the mud bottom of Bernie's memory like a stone.

When Bernie wasn't on her mind, Tory was. Wini called her several times, but Tory didn't pick up. Toward the end of the break, she finally returned one of Wini's calls. They chatted about nothing that mattered.

"Wini?" Tory said suddenly in a softer, higher voice.

"Yes?"

"You know when you first came to school?"

"Yeah?"

"You were different, you know? I mean, not like bad or anything. Just . . . different. I thought you were cool. Your own self. But with Calista and all, I couldn't . . . Well, I *didn't* tell you."

"Oh," said Wini, too shocked to utter more than a single syllable.

"But then you changed. You started looking and sounding just like everybody else. Like Calista, and Sam, and *me*. You treated your friend Bernie like a stranger. And he was so good to you! I even thought you might be getting a thing for Rob."

"Oh, well—"

"But I could have warned you about him. He broke my

heart, Wini, and that's the truth. I gave him my, well, I gave him everything, and the very next night he was out with somebody else."

"No!" cried Wini, who wasn't really shocked.

"That's why I left. I'm tired of the whole thing. Not just guys like Rob, but all the drinking and the partying."

"Are you coming back?" said Wini. "The room's so empty without you."

"Are you kidding?" Tory's laugh was harsh. "I only took one of my finals."

"You'd be on AP," said Wini.

"Not me. I'm going to start all over again at the community college here. Give myself a whole new start."

"Good for you," said Wini, echoes of her former self ringing in her ears.

"Let's keep in touch," said Tory. "And hey, get a better dye job, girl!"

\* \* \*

Wini began taking long, bracing walks by herself. She ate like a monk: brown rice, steamed veggies, tofu. She thought long and hard about many things. Now and then, she'd send Bernie an e-mail. Sometimes she'd attach a poem about life, the pain and the joy of it all. He hadn't written back, which worried her. How broken his heart must be. She walked alone in the zoo. It gave her strength for the road ahead.

At the end of the break when Wini boarded the plane, she looked pretty much like the redheaded, rosy-cheeked girl who'd left the first time, and seeing herself in the mirror was like meeting Winifred, an old friend.

# TWENTY ONE

Flying across the country, Winifred fidgeted in her seat. She couldn't wait to get to the university. Landing in Santa Barbara, Winifred collected her suitcase and waited impatiently for a taxi. She was focused. She was ready. If it wasn't too late, if Diedre hadn't cast the final spell on him, Winifred was going to get Bernie back.

In her alone hours at home, Winifred had taken many deep dives into her Self. Tory had only confirmed what Winifred already knew, deep inside. Somehow, in just a pitiful few months, she had become her own worst nightmare: a silly, vain, shallow, and deceitful person. Poor Bernie, trying his best to get her to open her eyes, even taking a class to impress her, got cast aside like last year's fashion mistake.

Well, no more. Wini was banished forever. Now Winifred Owens and Bernie Federman could start all over again, talk about real things: politics, poetry, life. They could dance like Ginger and Fred down the corridors of the library's eighth floor. Bernie was right all along. They belonged together, they always would.

Arriving at her old room, Winifred opened the door.

"Wini!" cried Calista and Sam in unison, like a couple of backup singers, their faces frozen in surprise.

"Your hair!" said Calista. "It's so . . . *red.*"

"It's really . . . different," offered Sam.

"It's mine," said Winifred, dropping her suitcase on the floor.

Calista frowned. "Are you gonna, like, wear those jeans? Here at school?"

"Yup," Winifred replied. "They're my favorites."

Calista and Sam exchanged a look as if to say: "Well, don't blame us. We did what we could."

"I guess you could come get a capp with us at the UCen, Wini," said Sam a little doubtfully. "We were just leaving."

Winifred smiled. "No, thanks. But could you guys do me a really big favor?"

Calista shrugged. "Sure."

"Call me Winifred, okay? That's my real name. Winifred."

\* \* \*

Bernie unwound Portia's leash from around his left ankle. Meanwhile, Peterkin and company had a field day running in five separate directions as far as their leashes would take them. Then they stood and gagged dramatically at passersby, as if to demonstrate what poor, abused (and darling) little dogs they were.

Bernie hadn't made much headway with the dogs, so walking them was always the dreaded part of his day. The real headway he'd made was on the essay for Diedre that he'd revised just this morning. Diedre had told him over coffee the week before that he had "a flair for the dramatic," which Bernie had decided was a good thing (he wasn't positive she meant it to be). He'd begun thinking about writing a novel again. It would be based on his life, sort of. More exciting than his real life, lots of dramatic things would have to happen. But that was the great thing about writing fiction. You could lie all you wanted and nobody would even know.

But novel writing was something he would have to do entirely on his own. Bernie's writing teacher at City College was no Diedre. He had introduced himself immediately as Dr. Shawcross in a way that let you know exactly how to approach him. The students would be doing a lot of research, he said, no "touchy-feely personal stuff."

Dr. Shawcross made Bernie miss Diedre. She and he had become friends. She had taken the truth, when at last he told it all, like a good friend would.

"You're eighteen?" she'd said. "You're kidding! I guess it's the nose that makes you look older. You *dog*, you!"

He apologized for standing her up, and then, bit by bit, told her all about Winifred and what a fool he'd been since arriving in Santa Barbara, sleeping on the library floor, scrounging for secondhand food, pretending to like her friends. As he told his story, Diedre's face went through so many changes that Bernie couldn't tell what was going through her mind. Was he an even bigger fool than he thought? Then, dabbing her eyes (from laughing? crying?), she'd said that thing about his flair for the dramatic.

It was such a relief to get the whole Winifred thing off his chest. Now, he told himself, he could really get on with his life.

Bernie began auditing Diedre's winter quarter UCSB class, which was already in full swing. The thought of running into Winifred—or any of her crowd—made Bernie hesitate, but Diedre had encouraged him to come. Winifred had e-mailed him over the break, and Bernie's foolish heart had leaped right up and begun to dance again. So he didn't write back. He couldn't. He missed Winifred something awful. He even missed Wini, sort of. Still, he didn't want to see her. Not now, not until he was stronger, and maybe not even then. He didn't trust himself not to fall into that old life again.

Peterkin decided his walk was done three blocks short of the house and wouldn't move. Finally Bernie stuffed the dog under his arm like a football and pulled the rest of the dogs home.

\* \* \*

Even though nobody was waiting to board, the cranky old library elevator stopped at every floor, sighing and giving a creepy little rattle before finally allowing its door to open. This gave Winifred just enough time to get rattled, too. It occurred to her as she stepped off the elevator onto the eighth floor that maybe, just maybe, Bernie wouldn't want to see her.

Could that be?

She pushed open the door to the Ancient East. The smell of fresh paint hit her head-on. Behind the bookcase that had once been Bernie's crash pad was nothing but a rolled-up canvas drop cloth and a giant can of industrial white.

Tears of panic sprang into Winifred's eyes. What an idiot she was. What had made her believe Bernie would be here anyway? Did she really think he never went anywhere else? That he had no other life? No other friends? Why had she expected that he'd be sitting monklike behind a bookcase, waiting for Winifred to come and save him?

But where had he gone? Not back to Pittstown. Bernie's father would have said something when she'd run into him at Rite Aid. Diedre, then. That had to be it. And there was only one way to find out.

\* \* \*

Bernie picked up the phone and dialed the number scribbled on a scrap of notebook paper. He let the phone ring twice and hung up.

What was wrong with him? Well, nothing. Nothing physical anyway. He thought about girls all the time. It was the best way to keep his mind off Winifred. There were girls at City College who were more interesting than Winifred and her friends, more mature, more serious about the future. And they seemed to regard Bernie differently than the UCSB girls did (*women*, Diedre kept reminding him, *women*). He had begun to catch one particular *woman* looking at him in class, openly, as if she might want to get to know him. And there were other women, too, women who smiled at him in passing.

Well, he looked better. He'd started to put on some weight, for one thing. But the difference was mostly his nose, which had healed with a tough-guy bend in it. It made him look older and just a little bit (he hoped) cruel.

He began to smile at perfect strangers. And he began thinking about dating, or at least asking somebody out for coffee, which was about all he could afford.

And then Cindy, the woman who looked at him in class, had struck up a conversation with Bernie after class. Something about the assignment, obviously just an excuse to talk. He'd almost asked her out on the spot, but then she'd given him her phone number before he could get up his nerve. All he had to do was call it. Bernie picked up the phone and dialed again.

\* \* \*

It was hard to respect someone with dead plants on their landing. Winifred knocked on Diedre's door. And then there was Diedre in the flesh. Well, in a pair of beat-up jeans, more or less like Winifred's. Her purple T-shirt said TAKE BACK THE NIGHT, a cause Winifred believed in, which made it hard not to like Diedre, which Winifred had decided to do.

"Hi," said Diedre. "Winifred? Come on in. I was just making myself a cup of chamomile tea. Would you care for some?"

"Oh, uh. No. No, thanks. I like your shirt though."

Diedre stood aside to let Winifred in. "You were in my class last quarter, right? Back row? So you're a friend of Bernie's?"

Winifred had called the day before, claiming to be an old friend of Bernie's from high school (true), saying she'd just found out through a mutual friend that Bernie was here at UCSB (untrue). But she didn't have an address or phone number for him (true). The mutual friend said Bernie had been auditing Diedre's class.

She hadn't counted on Diedre remembering her.

"Yeah, friends," said Winifred. "His parents and mine, well, they go way back." Winifred felt her face growing warm. The self she had so recently reclaimed hated lying, but if Diedre and Bernie were really having a "thing," she doubted Diedre would tell her where to find him.

"You're not in any hurry, are you?" Diedre said. "I think we should talk."

Like a canary in a coal mine, Winifred sensed danger. "I guess I'll have some tea after all," she said.

Diedre put two cups of hot water with tea bags in them on a tiny round table by the window. The table was half covered with open books piled facedown on top of each other. Winifred sat in one of the two spindly chairs. A spider plant (live) hung from a pot suspended from the ceiling, dripping baby spiders between her face and Diedre's. It was a little surreal, Diedre's face going in and out of spider shadow. Winifred wanted to bat the spiders away and say, "See here, Diedre. Here's the deal (thanks to Calista): Bernie's my man, get it? He's in love with me, and he always has been. So hand over the address and phone number and I'll be on my way."

Well, Bernie *had* been in love with her always, if four and a half years counted as always, which from a certain time-travel perspective, it certainly could.

Instead, Winifred meekly sipped her tea. Diedre intimidated her. If there was any woman in the world that Winifred would exchange lives with right now, it would be Diedre. Especially if she had snagged her Bernie. Diedre was smart, funny, attractive (in an exotic, thrift-store kind of way), and super-intelligent. She wouldn't fall for just any Saks makeup person claiming to know the latest tricks to really open those eyes (though it wouldn't hurt her if she did).

Wini had been intelligent once, light-years ago. Could she find her way back to Winifred? The girl who took Mensa quizzes for the sheer fun of it? Who thought calculus was a hoot?

"Since you're a friend of Bernie's, Winifred," Diedre said in a confidential tone, "I'm sure he wouldn't mind my telling you that he's recently come through a particularly rough time."

"He has," said Winifred. "I mean, he has?"

"The usual thing, I suppose," said Diedre. "He followed this girl out here from New Jersey . . . Did you say you were from New Jersey?"

"Right. Pittstown, New Jersey," said Winifred. She was glad for the dim light, for the spider shadows. Her face was burning up.

"And she, well, dumped him. Cold." Diedre shook her head, frowning as if she were seeing it all played before her on DVD. "And Bernie . . . Well, knowing him, you know how sensitive he is. For a while, he was a wreck. Absolutely lost."

"Oh!" cried Winifred, like a good friend would. "Poor Bernie!"

"But then—" Diedre dipped her tea bag several times and lifted it from the cup.

"Yes?" cried Winifred.

Diedre gave Winifred a smile, a smile Winifred couldn't interpret. "Well, she sapped his soul, you see." Diedre began winding the little string tighter and tighter around the tea bag, strangling the life out of it. "At last Bernie began pulling his life together. It wasn't easy. He told me it was like chewing glass." Diedre waited for Winifred's horrified reaction and smiled that cryptic smile again. "He began realizing where he was, for heaven's sake! How truly amazing this university is, how much it had to offer someone who was genuinely searching. You know? For someone with great intelligence who was on the point of selling himself out to something so far beneath him, a foolish chase after . . . well, nothing."

Diedre had been flinging her hands in space again, while the spider babies hung on for dear life. "He began clinging to literature like it was some kind of life preserver. And," she sighed again deeply, "he came through." She tossed the tea bag casually into the trash.

Winifred, who by now was hanging over the table, cried, "He did?"

"Oh, yes. Indeed he did. He's found himself a wonderful little studio downtown where he can begin writing in earnest, and he's even made some new friends. He's not looking back, believe me!"

"Oh," said Winifred, her heart a sodden little bundle somewhere in the vicinity of her liver.

"So," said Diedre, "when you see him again, if you do, well, you might be surprised. Bernie is a man, Winifred, not a boy. He's put childish loves and needs behind him. He's a whole new person. You might, in fact, not recognize him at all."

"Oh," said Winifred, looking down at Diedre's hand, which had somehow been laid, as if in comfort, on her own. A single tear escaped, trickling slowly down Winifred's cheek. She quickly brushed it away. "Allergies," she said, sniffing.

Diedre escorted Winifred to the door. "Bee pollen," she said as Winifred went out.

"What?"

"For those allergies," Diedre said, and closed the door.

It was several blocks before Winifred realized she still didn't have Bernie's address or even a phone number.

# TWENTY TWO

When the number 24 came to a stop in the bus circle and Bernie got off, the first thing he saw was the poster. You couldn't miss it, even though it was tacked to a kiosk filled with brightly colored flyers advertising upcoming campus events and notices for vacant or soon-to-be-vacant apartments.

WHOA, announced the poster in stark black print. Oddly familiar-looking print.

> Women! Are you saying NO
> and not getting heard?
> Men! Are you ready to help
> clean the campus of creeps
> who ruin your good name?
> Well, join the club.
> Come to UCen 202, Thursday,
> January 22, at 7:30 sharp.

The posters were everywhere. Sometimes with just the single word: WHOA, whatever that meant. Bernie walked all over campus, and whenever he saw another of the posters he stopped and smiled. He remembered the funny, brave eighth-grader in the green hat with the pom-pom and all the crazy ideas for clubs.

Well, good for Winifred, he said to himself. Good for her.

Bernie continued on his way to Diedre's class. They were reading the poetry of Philip Levine now. Philip was a man's man, yet he wasn't afraid to feel things. He didn't get paralyzed when love or, worse, a person you loved, died. He was philosophical, which was exactly what Bernie was trying hard to be. You had to rise above the mundane, keep your eye on the prize, and move on.

It was amazing to Bernie how poetry could teach you everything you needed to know about life.

Somewhere, there had to be a poem about girls who had the staying power of cheap deodorant. Which wasn't very romantic but, damn it, why couldn't he just forget about Winifred once and for all?

\* \* \*

For a while, in Winifred's mind, WHOA had stood for many things. It was the acronym she'd liked so much, and making it mean exactly the right thing wasn't easy. Women

Have Only Assets was lame. Women Helping Others Act was good but too generic; Women Helping Overcome Assault, also good but too specific. After all, Rob hadn't assaulted Tory, she'd been all too willing. He'd used her, and once he'd gotten what he wanted, he'd moved on to someone else.

Winifred finally settled for We Have Our Agenda, which the club didn't have as yet. But Thursday night, as she headed for the first meeting at the UCen, Winifred was filled with great ideas. Women, especially freshman women (freshwomen!), had to begin using their heads. If they were going to drink their faces off (and why not think about *that*?), at least they needed to serve as Designated Watchers for one another. And couldn't they come up with better things to do than party? How about a women's book club? A film circle? She was confident she could spark the minds of all her new members to come up with even better ideas.

WHOA had exactly three members. Herself and two other girls. But it was a start, and you had to start somewhere.

But not with Bernie.

Days passed. A week. Winifred tried not to think so much about Bernie. She threw herself into calculus and got an A on the first quiz. She changed her major to engineering. She went on long walks around the campus, attended a lecture on women and the visual arts. She took deep cleansing breaths and cold showers. She tried harder not to think about Bernie, but it wasn't working. A year ago when she thought he'd given up on life, she had sold him short. And here he was, going to classes he wasn't even getting credit for. Sure, they were Diedre's classes, but they weren't easy. By the time she was through with you, Diedre could make your brain *hurt*.

Unable to help herself, Winifred began sneaking into Diedre's contemporary American poets class, going early and taking a seat in the back row. For the hour that Diedre lectured, Winifred gazed mournfully at the back of Bernie's head and dreamed of a future in which, together, they looked back and laughed at all this.

Diedre knew Winifred was there, of course, but Winifred counted on Diedre to ignore her.

Which was foolish.

"And you in the back row," said Diedre toward the end of the hour on a cloudless Monday afternoon when Winifred had almost drifted off. "Yes, sorry I've forgotten your name. Wendy?"

Winifred's heart flew into her throat. She pointed at herself and lifted her eyebrows, as if to say, "You couldn't possibly mean me. I'm not even here!"

And then she caught on: Diedre was going to make Winifred squirm. Because Winifred had made Bernie suffer. She had known all along about Winifred and Bernie.

"Yes, you," barked Diedre. "The poet is so clear in that last line about final things. What do you make of it? He's closing the door, don't you think?"

"Um, yes?" said Winifred.

Bernie's head whipped around. His eyes widened. "Wow!" he said. "Winifred!"

A wave of titters ran through the class.

"Bernie," said Diedre. "It seems you have something to add."

Bernie had this goofy grin on his face he couldn't seem to do anything about. "I guess not," he said.

Winifred sat for the rest of the hour with her head down, reading the line "up my father's stairs" over and over again until it made no sense.

*He loves me, he loves me not . . .*

Still grinning, Bernie was waiting outside the classroom. "Wini!" he said the minute he saw her. "You look great! You're so pretty. How could I forget that? Your hair is . . . well, it's your *hair*!"

Winifred's mouth was dry. She couldn't speak. Her silly heart threatened to stop beating. Then it threw itself into high gear, leaving her breathless.

Bernie went on and on. "I mean, I know you were following the latest fashion and all that. But that purple eye stuff and those weird shoes and—"

"Bernie. Shut up. Please. Just stop."

Bernie stuffed his hands into the pockets of his windbreaker. "Right."

They began walking, slowly, toward the west end of campus. Bernie didn't take her hand. Winifred couldn't take his. She loved him so much there was no way to tell him, no simple way to say how she felt. Still, how she looked—now or before or twenty years from now—was entirely up to her. If she wore a burka or got a tattoo on her forehead it was her business, not anybody else's, not even Bernie's.

As if he'd rehearsed it beforehand, Bernie started talking about his new life, telling her all about his writer's studio, the dogs, his City College classes. "The thing is," he said at last, "I'm loving school. It's like I suddenly woke up. Like I'm some Rip Van Winkle character and the whole world got rearranged. Everything looks so different to me now. I'm going to be a writer, Wini."

"Winifred," she said sadly.

"I don't care where it takes me," he continued. Had he even heard her? "Or if it takes me anywhere. For the first time in my life, I know what I want, and it's so damned exciting!"

"I'm glad for you, Bernie," she said over the lump in her throat.

"And you," he said, winding down. "How's the old gang in 6C?"

"Fine," she said. "I guess." She told him that Tory was

going to a community college closer to home. Calista and Sam hadn't exactly raved about Winifred's changed appearance, but then she hadn't really expected them to.

"I've changed my major," she said. "I'm really headed toward nanoscience this time."

"That's so great, Wini. I—"

"Bernie? Will you please call me by my right name? I'm not Wini anymore. I hope I never have to hear that name again."

"You bet!" Bernie gave Winifred a quick, sideways squeeze. Then he stuck his hands back into the pockets of his windbreaker.

The bench near the edge of the cliff reminded Winifred of her first night on campus. How lonely and frightened she had been, but how determined, too, to make her college experience memorable. Well, she'd done that all right. How fast she'd slid down the slippery slope of mediocrity!

The bench reminded Bernie of the many times he'd sat all alone, convinced that sadness was a permanent fixture of his life. Once, he'd let himself break down, not giving a damn whether anybody heard his wretched, racking sobs. He coughed and cried out all the tears that he'd worked so hard to bury with his mother. After that, he could hear her laughter in his head again.

Today the ocean looked particularly blue, as if that was how it had meant to be all along. They sat side by side on the bench and Bernie took Winifred's hand, the hand he'd grabbed and trapped for the first time when they were four-teen. He turned it over, tracing her lifeline, a tiny frown creasing his forehead.

"It's too late, isn't it?" Winifred muttered into her lap. She swiped at her eyes with the cuff of her sweatshirt.

Bernie sighed. "I don't know, Winifred. The thing is, you were right."

"Right? I've never felt so wrong in my life."

"You said things had changed. I didn't want to believe it. I didn't even want to hear it. How could things change so fast, I kept asking myself."

Bernie smoothed the skin on the back of Winifred's hand with his thumb. "I thought for a while that, you know, maybe you never really loved me at all."

"Bernie!" cried Winifred with a look of horror. "I never stopped loving you, I didn't! I was just, I don't know, under some kind of spell or something." Then she frowned. "No, that isn't fair. It wasn't anybody else's fault. The girls never made me do anything I didn't want to do."

"Right!" he said. "I know. You got caught up in some-thing new and exciting. It happens." He shrugged. "It hap-pens."

"But it was all so stupid."

Bernie smiled a sad smile.

"Oh, Bernie," said Winifred as her tears branched into streams washing over her cheeks. "Do you think it was ever real, what we had?"

"As real as we are," he said. "You know it was, Winifred. We were everything to each other."

"Can't we still be?"

How pretty Winifred looked with her bright blue watery eyes and her red hair blowing in the cool January breeze.

"We can't," Bernie said. "We *shouldn't* be. We've both got to figure out who we really are first. Where we're going with our lives. What we want."

She shrugged. "That's easy. I want you."

"You want what we used to have, Winifred. I did, too. Wanted it so badly I couldn't see anything else." He shook his head, as if coming out of a trance. "I didn't even know who I was without you."

"Scary," she said as his words hit home.

"Yeah. Major scary."

Bernie put his arm around Winifred, pulling her into the place where she fit so well.

"What if I never find out who I am?" Winifred said after a while. "I mean it, Bernie. What if I'm, like, nobody? Underneath it all."

"Not possible, Winifred. You? You're one of a kind. You always have been. You just forgot that for a while. And me? I'm just waking up out of a long, bad dream. I can feel the creaky gears of my brain turning again."

"Bernie? Are we, like, breaking up?"

Tears clouded Bernie's vision. He blinked like crazy,

cleared his throat. "No! I mean, I know it feels that way, but—"

Winifred pulled away and looked at Bernie straight on. Her face was blotched and red. She sniffed and wiped her nose on her sleeve. "I love you, Bernie Federman," she said with the bravest smile she could manage. "I always will."

Bernie looked at the girl he once wanted more than his own life, knowing that he almost still did. He leaned over and kissed her. And kissed her. And then held her like a precious vase and kissed her some more. There was no denying it, kissing Winifred was the end of the drought, the sprouting seed, the open flower of spring. A poem he would never stop writing.

Winifred was weeping, or was it Bernie's tears running down both their faces? Kissing Bernie, she was kissing Bernie again! They were kissing like the world was ending.

Which it was, at least for them, if only for now.

A single cloud drifted across the blue canvas of the sky. A white dove swept down and landed on the bench beside Winifred. Except that it wasn't really a dove at all, just an ordinary seagull. Still, it had that knowing bird look in its eye.

"Bernie, do you think someday . . . ?"

Bernie nodded emphatically. "I do," he said.

"You do? Really?" Was the bench levitating, or was Winifred?

"Someday," Bernie said. "When it's right for both of us,

Winifred, I will probably do the most ordinary thing in the world. I'll get right down on one knee and ask you to marry me."

And then, out of nowhere, there was music, a swing band playing something sweet and sad and wonderfully romantic. But it could have been the wind.